I0694111

Many Mansions

This is a work of fiction set against a backdrop of real events. Any similarities between the characters and real people are unintended and coincidental

Chapbook Press

Schuler Books
2660 28th Street SE
Grand Rapids, MI 49512
(616) 942-7330
www.schulerbooks.com

www.edwardbloor.net

Many Mansions

ISBN 13: 9781966196488

Library of Congress Control Number: 2025922584

Printed in the United States by Chapbook Press.

For Pam, Amanda, and Spencer

Monday

The blue Mercedes convertible turned, very cautiously, off the smooth blacktop of Old Trail Drive onto the red clay of an unnamed road. The young woman at the wheel winced as the car's undercarriage scraped over the edge of the highway, dropped down, and settled into parallel lines of tire ruts. She reached over and lowered the transmission into D2, wishing she could, at the same time, lower the dueling voices shouting at her through the console, each voice speaking over the other like a long-married couple.

The crotchety male voice belonged to Mr. Charles MacDermott, her boss, who kept insisting, as he had been for the past thirty minutes, that she was on a fool's errand. "I told you, Richman! The crazy bastard is not out there. He's not out anywhere. He's dead!" The young female voice, one of two GPS options in the car, just kept repeating the word, "Recalculating," in a petulant monotone.

Janice Richman clutched the steering wheel and arched her back like a cat's, rising off the seat into the cool air as the male voice called out, "Are you there yet?" and the female one added, "Recalculating."

She rolled past an orchard of small peach trees, glowing pink in the sun, and came to a full stop before a metal gate. Her phone spat out the words, "Richman! Answer me! What the hell is going on?" which prompted a belated "Recalculating."

"A gate, Mister MacDermott. The road is blocked by a gate."

"Recalculating."

"Shut that damn thing off!"

"Yes, sir." Janice poked at the display, darkening the GPS screen.

"What's past the gate? What do you see?"

Janice peered over the windshield at a dirt road, dropping down a hillside, leading to a cluster of buildings. "I think this is it, Mister MacDermott. It's the Saint Francis Community."

"Damn. The place is still in business?"

"Yes, sir. It appears so."

"With damn monks and all?"

"Monks and nuns, at last count."

"Nuns?"

"Well, at least one."

"Damn. And you really think our nut-job could be living there? After all these years?"

"Possibly, sir. We've looked everywhere else."

The man exhaled angrily. "What a pain in the ass. Okay, get down there. If you find him, call me right away. We'll have to assemble the siblings, and they're not gonna like it."

"Yes, sir."

Janice climbed out into the mud and stepped slowly toward the gate, turning her feet sideways like a skier climbing a hill. She opened the gate with a light push and worked her way back, clenching her feet within her pumps to keep them from being sucked off. Then she dropped the car into D2 again and rolled forward to a precipice where the red clay road ended and the dirt one began.

One hundred yards away, a monk stood staring into the distance. When the blue car appeared, he focused on it with interest. He was a slender, fit-looking man, with bright red hair and a matching beard which provided a splash of color against his mud-brown robe and sandals.

He stood at the center of the St. Francis Community, a collection of five buildings, two farm plots, and a sprawling peach orchard. Directly behind him sat the largest building, a huge rectangle of sheet metal, ten thousand square feet inside, which served as a bakery and a shipping depot.

The monk turned away and busied himself, but he continued to watch as Janice climbed out of the blue car. She glanced into the side-view mirror and ran a quick hand through her dark curls. Then she grasped her iPhone and clutch purse and turned to face the sheet-metal building. She walked briskly across the compacted dirt until she reached a black circle of horse dung. Suddenly, she recoiled and jackknifed forward, as if she were about to vomit. She turned her face away and gulped at the air, managing to gain control of her gag reflex. She then righted herself to vertical, closed and opened her eyes two times, and continued on, giving the dung circle a wide berth. The monk, still following her every movement, sidled toward the building and positioned himself outside an open window.

Janice paused in the doorway. To her right, she saw a pair of industrial-grade ovens, a large stainless steel table, and two robed workers. In the back, she saw men in monks' robes working at other tables—unfolding flat red boxes, assembling them into cubes, and stacking them in rickety columns.

Janice stepped inside, feeling the heat of the ovens. She slid her iPhone into her purse and approached the robed figures, now identifiable as a man and a woman. The man was short and swarthy, with dark eyes set behind thick tortoise shell glasses. He wore the brown robe and sandals common to the members of the community, but his outfit appeared to be topped by an ill-fitting black toupee. The woman, similarly dressed, was very short and very thin, and she flitted hummingbird-like among the bowls of ingredients set out on the table. It was the woman who spotted Janice first. She snapped to a halt, narrowed her eyes, and called out in a voice tinged with challenge, "Can I help you?"

Janice apologized. "I am sorry to disturb you, but can I speak to the head man, the head *person*, of this . . ." she reached for the word, "operation?"

The short man stopped working and stared. His eyes seemed to drift behind his glasses, left to right, as if they were moving on their own. He answered before the woman could. "Operation? What? Are you are looking for a hospital?"

Janice replied, "No."

"Do you have a ruptured appendix or something?"

"No."

The woman shot her partner a withering look. She told Janice, in a no-nonsense voice, "You are looking for Brother Abelard. He's the abbot."

Janice nodded. "Yes. Yes, that sounds like exactly who I'm looking for."

The man snorted, "Well, you're not looking very hard. He's right there! Even I can see that."

The man pointed to a figure sitting at a card table against the left wall. Janice turned toward him as the woman shouted, "Brother Abelard! Brother Abelard!" in a voice intended to rouse him from sleep.

The figure opened his eyes and stared at Janice dully, like a hibernating bear. He struggled up out of his chair, rising to a height well over six feet; displaying a girth well over three hundred pounds. He was dressed in the same dark robe, but his was tied at the waist with a length of coarse rope. Janice started toward him, fearing that he could not walk, but he demonstrated that he could and met her at the doorway. Janice caught a whiff of the manure pile and started to gag again, but she artfully turned it into a yawn, saying, "I am so sorry. I've been driving since six A. M."

The big man asked, in a sonorous voice, "Ah. Driving from where?"

"Richmond."

"Ah." The man held out his hand and Janice took it, moving it up and down one time in a soft shake. He said, "I am Brother Abelard, the Abbot of Saint Francis. Are you here for a fruitcake?"

"Pardon me."

"A Saint Francis Community Fruitcake. The gift that's not just for Christmas anymore, made with our own home-grown Virginia peaches?"

"Uh, sure. All right. I'll take one."

"What about a hand-hewn crucifix or rosary?"

"Oh. No."

"Or a Saint Joseph statue. Also hand-carved?"

"I don't think so. I'm Jewish."

"Ah, I see." He pointed out, "Well, so was Joseph. And some Jewish people purchase his statue for real estate purposes."

"What?"

"They bury the statue of Saint Joseph in the front yard of a house that has not sold in a long time and, suddenly, miraculously, it sells."

"Really?"

"So they tell me. They're a popular item. And they're hand-hewn. Will you take one?"

"No. No."

"Well then," he looked toward the table, "Sister Agnes, please get one fruitcake for . . . Miss? Missus?"

"Miss. Richman. Janice Richman."

"Ah."

The little nun took off as Janice said, "Sir, Abbot, I'll get right to the point. I am trying to find someone. His name is Rowan James Butler. He wandered away from Appomattox College twenty years ago, and I thought he may have wandered over here."

The abbot's eyes blinked rapidly. His brow furrowed. He replied, "That's doubtful. Most doubtful."

Janice pressed him. "But, obviously, he had to go *somewhere*, and this community was within walking distance."

"Of Appomattox College? Hardly."

Janice stared down at his ample stomach. "Of course, Mister Butler would have been younger then. And perhaps, with the energy of a younger man, you know . . . ."

The abbot murmured, "Mister Butler?" Then he explained, "We leave our secular names behind when we enter the monastic life, choosing monastic names."

"Yes, but you must have records of when people first arrived and had those, you know, secular names."

"Ah, yes. I suppose we must."

Suddenly, Janice's phone sprang to life with a peppy xylophone ring, displaying MacDermott's number. Janice's eyes bulged out in apology. She held up one finger and turned around. She clicked the phone on inside the purse and whispered, "I'm speaking to the abbot right now, Mister MacDermott."

"The who?"

"The head monk."

"Oh. All right. Let's get this thing over with, huh?"

"Yes, sir."

Janice clicked off and explained, "I represent the law firm of MacDermott and Richman. We are attempting to execute the will of two of our clients who have, unfortunately, passed away. We are trying to locate their heirs."

Brother Abelard nodded solemnly. "We have a perpetual prayer card that may interest you then."

"What? What's that?"

"It's the sympathy card with a difference. It informs a family that this community will remember their deceased loved one in our daily prayers for perpetuity."

"Oh, well—"

"Was the deceased Jewish?"

"No. As I said, there are *two* deceased, but neither was Jewish."

"You would like two cards then?"

Janice conceded, "Sure. Okay."

At that moment, the little nun returned carrying a red box stamped with the words: *St. Francis Community Fruitcake*. She handed it to Janice, who reacted to its surprising weight by whispering, "Whoa."

Brother Abelard informed the nun, "Miss Richman will also take two perpetual prayer cards, Sister."

The nun rolled her eyes, turned on her heels, and hustled to a back corner of the cavernous room.

Brother Abelard said, "All right, Miss. If I may, I will research this matter in the office building, where we keep all of our records. I will leave you in the capable hands of Brother Carl here. He can explain to you how we make the fruitcake." The big man then turned slowly and ponderously, like a ship in port, and exited the building.

Brother Carl called over. "Yeah, sure. I'll tell you all about it! What do you want to know?"

Janice tried to smile. "Okay. Well, what are you doing now?"

"It's Monday, so we're making dough. We make dough on Monday, Tuesday, and Wednesday; we bake on Thursday and Friday; we ship on Saturday. What else do you want to know?"

She shook her head. "Nothing really. You go ahead and . . . make dough."

"Come on. Come over here where I can see you."

Janice approached the near side of the table, set the red box down, and looked at him, prompting him to snap, "What? What are you staring at? My toupee?"

"No. No."

"There's no vow against wearing a toupee. I looked it up. There's nothing about toupees."

"All right."

"No tonsure here. No mandatory bald heads. Not a word about it." He waited for Janice to speak. When she did not, he elaborated. "We do take vows, serious religious vows, when we join the Community. But there's no toupee vow, so everybody better get over that. Maybe I have to be short and ugly, but I don't have to be bald."

Sister Agnes re-appeared. She paused a moment to shake her head disapprovingly at Brother Carl. Then she handed Janice two oversized cards and envelopes. Each card bore the words: *Perpetual Prayers for Your Loved One* in flowing black calligraphy. The little nun pointed to a blank line on the top card. "That's where *you* fill in the name of each deceased."

Janice took hold of the cards and envelopes. "Okay."

The nun then handed her a small index card and a pen. "Here. *We* need to know the names of the deceased, too."

Brother Carl called over. "Yeah. How else would we know who to pray for? Are we supposed to say: *And please remember blank?*"

Janice did as she was told as the nun explained, in an efficient monotone, "We will begin remembering them today, at the Mid-day Prayers." Janice handed the index card and pen back. Sister Agnes then reached into her robe, produced a small black calculator, and summarized, "So! You are purchasing these three items. Will there be anything else?"

"No."

"The perpetual prayer cards are fifty dollars each—"

"Really? Fifty dollars? For a card?"

"They are *perpetual*, Miss. Do you know what that means?"

"Yes."

"We pray for these people forever. Our time is surely worth something. Is it not?"

"Yes."

"And thirty-five dollars for the fruitcake." The nun poked at the calculator. "Plus five-point-three percent Virginia state sales tax, plus one percent local tax comes to one hundred forty-three dollars and fifty cents. Will that be cash?"

"No. Sorry. I don't carry much cash."

"Credit or debit?"

"Credit, I suppose. Do you take American Express?"

The nun stashed the calculator and replied coldly, "American Express is guilty of usury. Do you know what that is, Miss?"

"No. I guess n—"

"The sin of greed, charging excessive interest. We take Visa and MasterCard."

"Okay. MasterCard."

Janice dug into her purse, found the correct card, and handed it over. Sister Agnes took off again. Janice looked despairingly toward the front door. Brother Abelard was nowhere in sight. Her gaze drifted to the open window, where she saw a monk's face looking back at her. She registered two facts about him immediately: He had blue eyes, and he had red hair.

Sister Agnes returned with an old-fashioned credit card imprinter and swiped a form over Janice's card. "Sign that, please."

Janice took the proffered pen and signed. The little nun tore off the bottom-most copy and handed it to her, saying, "Here is your receipt."

"Thank you." Janice pointed to the window. "Can you tell me? Who is that standing in the window?"

The nun followed Janice's gaze; she answered flatly, "That's Brother Thomas."

"Oh? He doesn't make fruitcake?"

Carl interrupted. "Who? Him? No. Not him. I guess he's too smart now." He frowned and added, "He used to be too nuts to work; now he's too smart. Go figure."

Sister Agnes addressed Janice. "No one here calls him nuts."

Brother Carl insisted, "Oh no? Well, he walks like a nut. He sleeps like a nut, too."

Sister Agnes dismissed him with, "I wouldn't know," and turned back to Janice. "He *does* work on fruitcake sometimes. During the Christmas rush season. Everybody pitches in then."

Brother Carl pointed to Janice, but he spoke to the nun. "She don't care about making fruitcake."

Janice protested mildly, "I wouldn't say that."

Brother Carl again addressed his colleague. "I started to tell her about it, but she looked away. Maybe *you* should try."

The little nun replied coldly, "And why would I do that, Brother?"

"Because Brother Abelard said to."

"Oh." Sister Agnes's voice changed to a warmer one. She told Janice, "We make real, old-fashioned fruitcakes for the holidays and for any other time of the year. We use our own farm-fresh butter, sugar, and eggs. We grow almost everything here."

Carl added, "Yeah. Except for what we don't grow here. We go out and buy that at Wal-Mart. And the people stare at us."

The nun ignored him. "We use our own peaches. Did you see the peach trees when you were driving in?"

"Yes!"

Carl conceded, "Okay. We grow the peaches here." He pointed to the red box. "I thought of a motto to put on the fruitcake boxes, but Brother Abelard said *no*. He said it was passive aggressive. Do you know what that means?"

"I do."

"Do you want to hear the motto?"

Janice glanced toward the window. She muttered, "Sure."

"*Give your family what it truly deserves—a fruitcake.*" He held out his hands in supplication. "Do you see anything wrong with that?"

Janice didn't reply.

"What are you staring at now? My eyes?"

Janice was indeed looking at the little man's eyes behind his thick lenses. His pupils seemed to move independently of each other, floating like olives in a martini glass. He told her, "Do you want to know what it's called? It's called *large-angle strabismus*. Deal with it. I do."

Janice looked down and an awkward silence ensued. Sister Agnes set to work at the table, flattening small clumps of dough with loud whacks from a wooden mallet. Brother Carl watched her for a moment; then he turned to Janice and asked, in a conciliatory tone, "So, you said you're from Richmond."

Janice nodded. "Yes."

"You were born there?"

"No. I was born and raised in Savannah."

"I don't know Savannah. I know Richmond pretty good, though. I drive over there a lot."

"Really? You drive?"

The monk's anger returned immediately. "Sure. Why shouldn't I?

Who are you, the Department of Motor Vehicles?"

Janice raised up both shoulders. "No."

"Brother Abelard lets me drive whenever I want. He won't let me take the Ford Ranger, but he lets me take the Corolla, whenever I want."

Sister Agnes added, "You shouldn't drive anything. Because you can't see anything."

"I can see! I can see good enough to drive."

The two squared off across the table, in what seemed to be the resumption of an ongoing fight. Janice stole another glance at the office building.

Brother Carl snarled, "At least I'm not a drive-by killer like you." He turned to include Janice. "She runs over turkeys with the truck! She kills them with a truck. Then *we* have to eat them."

Sister Agnes replied, "What does it matter how we kill them?"

"It matters because I don't like eating rubber tires with my turkey." He pointed at Janice. "And the turkeys are the *lucky* ones! They die right away. It's quick. But the deer? She'll run down a deer with the pickup truck and break its legs!"

The nun protested, "Oh nonsense. The deer gets stunned for one moment; then I finish it off with the shotgun. It's quite humane."

"Humane!"

"More so than you blasting away at them, killing anything that moves." She returned to banging dough, but she quickly added, "If you don't like the thought of killing animals, Brother, then don't eat meat."

Janice turned back to the window. The monk with the red hair was still there; still focused on her.

Brother Abelard's massive frame suddenly filled the doorway. He strode over to Janice and reported confidently, "There has never been anyone named Rowan James Butler here at Saint Francis."

"Are you sure?"

"Yes. Quite sure. I went back over the records for the past thirty years."

Janice pointed at the man outside. "Who is that? With the red hair?"

The big man turned slowly and looked. He replied, "Him? Oh, no. No, that is Brother Thomas." Then he repeated, as if it were the last word on the subject, "*Thomas*; not that other name."

"But Thomas is just his monk name, right?"

"What?"

"That's his name here at the Saint Francis Community, right? Thomas?"

"Yes, it is. That is Brother Thomas."

"I realize that. But what was his name when he arrived here?"

"Oh, I don't know."

Janice looked despairingly at the open doorway. She asked, "Could you please go check?"

"Oh, I checked. Just now. I looked at all the names of the novitiates for the last thirty years."

Janice pointed at the window. "Well, what was that man's name?"

"Who?"

"That one! Thomas!"

"Ah. Well, yes, I do recall now. Brother Thomas's name was John."

"John what?"

"It was John Smith."

Janice challenged him, "Oh come on. John Smith?"

The abbot did not appear to be offended. He explained calmly, "Many people *are* named John Smith, Miss. Especially here in Virginia. There are well over fifty-thousand John Smiths in the United States!"

Janice had heard enough. She told him, "Sir, Abbot, Brother Abelard . . . I need to have a short conversation with Brother Thomas about an important legal matter."

"Ah. What matter is that?"

"Whether his non-monk name is—"

The monk suddenly rapped his knuckles against the windowpane three times, startling Janice, and causing Sister Agnes and Brother Carl to stop their work. He then disappeared from the window and reappeared in the open doorway. He pointed at Janice: then he pointed up the road and took off walking at a brisk pace, clenching and unclenching his fists and working his cheek muscles, as if counting each step.

Janice concluded, out loud, "That's Rowan James Butler. Isn't it?"

Brother Abelard insisted, "No. That's Brother Thomas." He hastily added, "The former John Smith."

"Then why is he pointing at me and running away?"

Brother Abelard explained, "He is not! Brother Thomas, I assume, has spotted a wild turkey or some other regional fowl that he hopes to capture and prepare for the evening meal."

Sister Agnes sprinted around the table and shouted through the doorway, "Brother Thomas! You can't do this! You took a vow!"

Brother Carl remained at the table, but he shouted after him, too. "You took a vow, you bum! You nut-case! Get back here!"

Sister Agnes repeated the words, "You took a vow!" Then she ran to the abbot and asked breathlessly, "Can I take the Ranger and go after him?"

Brother Abelard nodded. "Yes. Just be sure to use the sign-out sheet." Sister Agnes bolted out of view around the right side of the building.

Janice took off, too, running in her heels until she reached the dirt outside, whereupon she walked quickly. She fished out her keys and started the engine from ten feet away. She slid in, threw the transmission into D2, and peeled away from the building. She quickly pulled up even with the red-haired monk, who was walking resolutely along the side of the road. She slammed on her brakes and called out, "What is your name?" When he did not reply, she repeated, "Your name? Your real name. What is it? Are you Mister Rowan James Butler?"

He nodded rapidly; affirmatively. Janice pointed to the passenger seat and told him, "Then get in."

Without hesitation, the monk slid his buttocks onto the top of the door, pivoted his legs around, and dropped down into the seat, introducing a whiff of horse dung that nearly overpowered Janice.

"Oh! Agh!"

The monk noticed her discomfort, pulled off his sandals, and clapped them together outside the window, removing mud and manure. The blue car accelerated all the way back to the open gate before Janice could speak. She braked to a halt and said, "Mister Butler. I represent the law firm of MacDermott and Richman." He nodded impatiently, turning to check if someone was in pursuit. "Do you . . . Do you want to leave the grounds with me right now, Mister Butler?"

He nodded *yes*.

"But. What about your belongings?"

He shook his head *no*.

"Well, I'll need something from you. A photo ID of some kind. Some paperwork."

He shook his head *no* again.

"No? You have nothing like that?"

Another shake *no*.

"But then . . . How can I know who you are?"

He leveled a blue-eyed stare at her. Then he spoke, in a soft and intelligent voice, "That's a good question."

Janice gasped. "You talk?"

"Of course I talk. I'm not dumb."

"Well, no. Sorry."

"We're not a silent order. You've been talking with the others for twenty minutes."

Janice gulped. "All right then." She chose her words carefully, "Well, Mister Butler, it is my sad duty to inform you that both your parents are deceased."

The monk nodded. "Yes. I heard everything you said back there; I heard you through the window."

Before Janice could reply, her xylophone ring sounded. She made a face—half apology, half *I need to get this*—and activated the phone on the car console. They both heard MacDermott snarl, "Did you find the crazy bastard or not?"

"Uh, yes, sir."

"What's going on?"

"He's right here with me. In the car."

"Oh. Are you sure it's him?"

"Reasonably sure, sir."

"Well, does he have any ID?"

"No. He has no possessions at all, Mister MacDermott. Just the clothes on his back."

"So how do we know who he is?"

"I asked if him if he was Rowan James Butler, and he nodded."

"He could be a junkie. They nod all the time."

"He's not a junkie." She added, "He can hear you, by the way."

MacDermott was undeterred. "He could be crazy. Ask him if he's George Washington."

Rowan glared at her.

"No. He says, he *indicates*, no."

"All right. We'll pursue identification just like we would for a dead man—fingerprints, DNA, that sort of thing. I'll set it up on this end."

"Yes, sir."

"Does he look anything like his mother?"

"I don't know, sir. What did she look like?"

"She had wavy red hair, blue eyes, very white skin."

Janice shot a sideways glance at her passenger. "Yes, sir. I'd say *yes* to all three. I'm pretty sure we have our man."

"Well I'm not. Send me a photo. Now."

Janice pulled the iPhone out of her purse, raised it, and snapped a picture of the startled-looking monk. She keyed in MacDermott's name and sent it off.

He replied within seconds with just one word: *Damn.*

The GPS voice instructed Janice, "Turn right on Jarmin's Gap Road."

Rowan stared at the console, and then at Janice. He asked, "Whose voice is that?"

"No one's. It's just . . . a voice. The female GPS voice."

Rowan considered her answer and then replied, "She sounds like a robot."

"Yes, I suppose she does."

The voice instructed her, "Turn left on Greenwood Station Road."

Rowan muttered, "People have robots now." He leaned to his right, hunched down, and stared into the side mirror. Not satisfied with his view, he turned so that his knees were on the seat cushion and he could stare directly out the back window.

After a few seconds, Janice told him, "We're getting onto the highway, Mister Butler. You really should put on your seatbelt."

The monk twisted around until he was forward-facing; then he plopped down. He admitted, "Uh, I'm not sure how to do that."

Janice did a double take. She told him, "Reach up, over your right shoulder, and pull the metal clip out and down." When Rowan did as asked, she added, "Now stick that metal end into the clicky thing, down there by your left hip."

"Clicky thing?"

"It has a red button on it."

"Oh. Yes."

Rowan followed her instruction. Janice smiled when she heard the clicking sound. She asked him, "When's the last time you rode in a car?”

“It’s been a long while.”

“Didn’t the car have seat belts?”

“Yes, I suppose it did. But they weren’t like this.”

“Uh huh.”

The xylophone sound returned, followed by the voice of MacDermott. “Richman! Pick up!”

Janice reached into her purse, clicked on the phone, and held it up to her ear. “Yes, sir.”

“Are we speaking privately?”

Janice stole a glance at her passenger and answered, “Yes.”

“First of all, where the hell is your father?”

“I don’t know, sir.”

“No. Nobody does. I doubt if he does! I had to call those damn Butler siblings myself.”

“Yes, sir.”

“I hate those two.”

“Yes, sir.”

“Let’s just say they are very skeptical about this man you found. So I’ve got a company called LabTech ready to certify that this guy is either Rowan James Butler or a hairy nut-job. I’m hoping for hairy nut-job.”

“Why?”

“So Kitty Butler won’t have a shit fit in my office tomorrow morning.”

“She probably will anyway.”

“Listen: I’m looking at the picture you sent me of this guy, and he looks like a goddamn orangutan. We can’t have *that* sitting in our meeting room. Can you stop someplace and clean him up?”

Janice glanced at her passenger. “How would I do that, sir?”

“I don’t know. You’re the girl. Get him shampooed? Get his hair cut?”

Janice stole another glance. “It’s not like I found a dog, Mister

MacDermott."

"No. You found an orangutan. Now get him cleaned up. And get rid of that beard."

Janice considered the problem, then she answered, "Well, I do have a friend. Laurence Myers."

"What does he do?"

"He owns Nola's Salon in the Designer Fashion Park. He could help with a cleanup; probably with a whole new look. He specializes in new looks."

MacDermott spoke as if to himself. "I don't know what that means, but okay. Do it." He told her, "I'll have the lab guy meet you at that Nola's Salon. He'll take a hair sample."

"Then what happens?"

"We see if it's a match."

"A match to what?"

"Rowan Butler's mother left behind a baby book. It's got one of those *Baby's First Haircut* pages. She left behind a hairbrush, too, with her own hair in it. We can match the sample to either one. Or not."

"All right."

"And can you get him some decent clothes? Something from this millennium?"

"Yes, sir. There are clothing stores at the Fashion Park. Laurence used to dress the reporters at WTVR."

"He dressed them? What does that mean?"

"He picked out their clothes. For when they went on the air."

MacDermott muttered, "Nice work if you can get it."

"Yes, sir." She asked him, "Now, what is the budget for all this?"

MacDermott exhaled. "The budget is whatever you need to spend to get the job done. Use the American Express card."

"Yes, sir. If you say so."

"I say so. Don't scrimp. If you show up here with the Missing Link, Kitty might really lose it."

MacDermott hung up in the middle of a final, "Yes, sir" from Janice. She looked at her phone screen, said, "Huh," and put it away.

Rowan asked, "Did you say you have a friend who is going to *clean me up*?"

"Yes. Well, we need to improve your . . . personal appearance, Mister Butler."

"Why?"

"We need to make you look like the heir to a great fortune. Otherwise, your family members may contest the will."

"My family members? Who would those be?"

"Your half-siblings, Kitty and Ewell Butler."

Rowan thought for a moment, then said, "Kitty. She's kind of nasty, right?"

"From what I hear."

"And what about Ewell?"

"Well, my dad calls him *Ewell the Tool.*"

"What does that mean?"

"I guess it means he's a dick. Or maybe a dickhead, in this case." Rowan appeared to be puzzled. Janice said, "All I know is what my dad told me: Kitty and Ewell thought you were dead. They thought you had," she paused, but then continued, "committed suicide in college."

"Why would they think that?"

"They—and by *they* I mean Kitty, Ewell, their attorneys, and a detective agency—drew that conclusion based on the information they had."

"What information?"

"Medical records from Appomattox College. An investigation by the detective agency. And the fact that you did not re-surface for all these years."

Rowan nodded slowly, and then he went silent for the rest of the drive.

At noon, Janice turned into the Designer Fashion Park and cruised until she saw the sign: *Nola's Salon.* She pulled to the curb across from the front door and texted her boss that she had arrived. Then she spoke to Rowan for the first time in over an hour. "I wonder who Nola is."

Rowan answered, "I don't expect there is one. It's a palindrome."

Janice replied tentatively, "Uh huh. What's that again?"

"It's a phrase that reads the same forward and back, like: *Madam, I'm Adam.* In this case, *Nola's Salon.*"

"Oh. Okay. Got it." Janice looked up at the salon window and saw a thin man, with henna-red hair, staring at her. He was dressed in a sparkling white polo shirt and khaki board shorts. He gave her a sly wave. She said, "That's Laurence! He and I went to the same schools together, for like twelve years."

"He's your friend?"

Janice paused. "I'd say he's more of a frenemy."

"What's that?"

"He can be a friend or an enemy, depending on his mood."

"That's a portmanteau word."

"What is?"

"*Frenemy.* It's a word formed by folding two words together, like the folding sides of the suitcase known as a portmanteau."

"Oh."

"Like *smoke* and *fog,* folded together, make *smog.*"

"Got it."

Rowan observed, "He appears to be a homosexual."

Janice stared at her passenger for a moment and then replied, "Well, he is gay, yes."

"We have homosexuals at the Community."

Janice said, "Interesting." Then she pulled out her phone and texted a message to the man in the window: *Laurence?*

He replied right away: *Is that my favorite fag hag?*

She texted: *Come out please.*

He replied: *I came out in fifth grade, honey.*
Come out to my damn car, Laurence!
The little blue car?
Yes.
With the muddy red undercarriage?
Yes.
Who's that with you?
Come find out.

Laurence pushed open the door and strolled out. Janice could now see that he was very tan, and he had supplemented his look with a metal neck chain and boat shoes. She rolled down the window to air kiss with him. He bent over and stared across at her passenger, whispering, "I wanted to make sure you weren't with some pervert. Or with some unattractive pervert."

"Can you please help me, Laurence? I'm desperate."

"I can see, honey. So desperate you've gone paleo. Now who is he?"

Janice gritted her teeth. "He's a client. This is Rowan James Butler. I have to get him cleaned up, dressed, and styled for a very important meeting this afternoon. Can you do it?"

"You know I can. But you'll have to stop calling me Laurence."

"Why?"

"I'm Lance now."

"Lance?"

"Yes. The name, the henna hair, the tan—they all make a strong surfer statement, don't you think?"

"You surf?"

"Heavens no. It's my new look." He stepped back so she could take him in. "Come on! I've changed my look again. You didn't even notice?"

Janice claimed, "I did. Of course." She added, "I like it."

He muttered, "That was grudging."

"Why *Lance*?"

"Do you have to ask? And it has worked wonders. Like back in college, when I changed from *Lawrence* with a *w* to *Laurence* with a *u.* It's been transformational. I now move in a whole new world."

She told him, "Well, that's exactly what Mister Butler needs: *transformational.*"

Lance stared at Rowan's red hair. "That color is to die for." He winked at Janice, as he asked Rowan, "So . . . Who does your head?"

Rowan replied, "Pardon me?"

"Who cuts your hair?"

"I cut it myself."

"I believe you. With a tomahawk?"

"What?"

Lance rapped his knuckles against the car door. "All right; come inside. Ian is available now." He lowered his voice, "Frankly, Ian is always available." He pointed at Janice's Gucci purse. "How are you paying? And how *much* are you paying?"

"Mister MacDermott said to spend whatever it takes; he said not to scrimp."

"I like the sound of that. In cash?"

"No."

"You still don't carry cash?"

"I carry a sensible amount. Twenty dollars."

Lance sighed. "Yes, and you wear sensible shoes." He reached into his board shorts and pulled out a fat roll of bills.

Janice asked him, "And you still carry dangerous amounts?"

"Absolutely. This is a cash business. The tipping part, anyway. I'll front you five hundred for openers."

"Five-hundred dollars!"

"It's not like it's your money."

"All right. All right. I'll go park."

He told her, "No. Leave the car."

"What? Here?"

"Yes. It's salon parking. People do it all the time."

Somewhat reluctantly, Janice exited the car and gestured to Rowan to do the same. He climbed out, walked around to the front in his measured gait, and stopped. He remained in place, not moving, prompting Lance to start tapping one boat shoe up and down on the pavement impatiently.

Rowan pointed to the salon. He said, "I don't know what's happening. Why are we going in here?"

Janice answered patiently, "I told you. We need to clean up your look."

"But why?"

"So that things will go smoothly, and you'll get your inheritance, and the siblings won't contest it."

Rowan considered her words. "But what do you care?"

Janice looked genuinely puzzled. "What?"

"What do you care who gets this inheritance? It's not going to be you. Right?"

"Right." Janice shot a quick look at Lance and then answered. "Okay. I care because my father may have dropped the ball on this case. And I want to help him."

"Dropped the ball? What does that mean?"

"He was supposed to find you, but, I don't think he tried very hard to do that."

Lance called over, "We'll be closing soon, ladies!"

Janice continued, "So I found you. I did it to . . . help him."

"So this is about your father as much as it is about me, some strange monk you found in a field?"

"Yes. Yes, I suppose you could say that."

Rowan nodded. "That I can understand." He finally stepped up onto the pavement. Lance made an elaborate show of opening the door, and then he followed Janice and Rowan into the salon.

As soon as he entered, Rowan recoiled before a cloud of scents, covering his nose with both hands. A half dozen black-clad workers turned and stared at him and his long robe and sandals. Rowan stared back at a tableau of flamboyantly dyed hair, piercings, and tattoos.

Lance announced, "Ladies and gentlemen, I give you *Encino Man!* Recently discovered in a block of ice." When no one reacted; he added, with annoyance, "Don't you remember? Brendan Fraser? Anyone?"

Janice whispered, "We're kind of in a hurry, Laurence."

He corrected her, "Lance," and pointed to a seated man reading a magazine. "Ian, darling! Surf's up! This one is all yours."

A wiry, tattooed man with a shaved head stood and asked, "Encino Man was a cave man, right? What am I supposed to do with a cave man?"

Lance handed him a hundred-dollar bill. "Wash and cut his hair. And remove his beard."

Ian looked concerned. He stared at Rowan's long main of hair and asked, "Has he taken a bath?"

Lance replied, "I don't know. Let's ask him."

Everyone looked at Rowan, waiting for him to speak. He finally managed, "Yes, I bathe."

Lance muttered, "Hmm. That word is, somehow, not reassuring. I'm thinking once a week, in a washtub, with a bar of lye soap. I am also hearing banjo music."

Ian pocketed the money and led Rowan into the back area of the salon, where he directed him to sit back in a reclining chair and rest his head in a sink.

Lance put his arm around Janice and turned her away so that they were both looking into a mirror. He said, "I think you've gotten shorter, darling. You've certainly gotten skinnier."

"Let's call it leaner. I'm working out."

He shook his head sadly. "But you are still rocking the pink nail polish?"

"Yes."

"And the lipstick?"

"Yes. Why not?"

"Because you're not Sandra Dee, and this isn't *Tammy Tell Me True*." He squeezed her hip. "Such a lean girl. Such a pretty girl. Why don't you have a husband?"

Janice broke free from his grip. "I don't know. Why don't you?" She looked him up and down and added sarcastically, "Really? Surf's up?"

Lance regarded himself in the mirror as he spoke. "You missed last winter's look—Nordic ski bum with white hair. I even learned some Swedish." He made a comical bow and asked, "Vad heter du?"

"How's that?"

"What is your name?"

"Oh."

A large van bearing the words *LabTech* pulled up in front of the door. A dark-skinned man in a bright red *LabTech* shirt hopped out and entered the salon. Janice held up one finger to him and asked Lance, "Oh yes! This man needs a hair sample. Can we do that?"

Lance glanced toward the back. "Can it be from the floor?"

"I think so. Yes."

Lance popped up one thumb and told her, "Inga problem."

"What? Who's Inga?"

"Ha! Nobody, darling. That's Swedish for *no problem*." He looked about. "Now, what should I put his lovely locks in?"

"Do you have an envelope?"

"I have gift certificates. And they have envelopes."

"That will do."

Lance walked behind the cash register, fished around, and located a long gold envelope. He carried it to the back, scooped the floor next to Rowan's chair, and returned with a tuft of red hair. Janice took the envelope, tucked in the flap, and handed it to the driver, who exited as quickly as he had entered.

When the van pulled away, though, it revealed a troubling sight to Janice. A *Virginia State Police* car was now parked behind her blue

Mercedes, and a state trooper was making note of her license plate.

Janice pointed outside and kept pointing until Lance turned to see the police car. He grimaced and muttered, "Oh dear."

"You said to park it there! You said it was salon parking!"

He replied, "It is. Come on. I'll take care of it."

The trooper was short and broad-shouldered. He had bronze skin and sharp, angular features. He looked up and asked in a clipped, no-nonsense voice, "Is this your car?"

Janice stammered, "Yes, sir."

"Then I'll need to see your license and registration."

Lance spoke up brazenly. "What do you care where she parks? You're state police. You need to be out on the highway . . . catching interstate sex traffickers or something."

The trooper answered evenly, "I need to be in here at the moment, sir. And this car is blocking the road."

Lance tried, "People park here for one minute, just for emergency pick ups. Like, people who have had intense salon work done."

The trooper responded with skepticism. "Intense salon work? Really? What is that?"

"Deep muscle massage. New-Age Rolfing. That sort of thing. Some people can't even walk after."

"New-Age Rolfing? I've never heard of that."

Lance explained, "It's like a massage, except very painful." When the trooper didn't respond, Lance added, "You can come in for a demonstration if you like."

The trooper raised his sunglasses. He met Janice's brown eyes with a pair of hazel ones. "Is that the case here, Miss? Did you drop someone off for an emergency, painful massage?"

Janice answered honestly, "No. No, sir. But I *did* drop someone off. And it *was* on important legal business. I work for the law firm of MacDermott and Richman, and there has been a death. There have been *two* deaths."

The trooper tore off a ticket, said, "I'm sorry to hear that," and handed it to Janice. She scanned the numbers on it.

Lance asked her, "How much is the fine?"

The trooper answered. "If you pay right away, it's one hundred fifty-five dollars."

Lance replied, "Well, how about if I pay right away?" He peeled off two hundred-dollar bills and extended them to the trooper.

The trooper returned his glasses to the bridge of his nose and glared at the money. He said, "Are you attempting to bribe an officer of the law?"

"No! Heavens no! You said if we paid now—"

"You pay the County Clerk. By check or credit card."

Janice read from the ticket. "Trooper Dan Bateman. Now, is that a Jewish name?" The trooper did not reply. After a moment, Janice exhaled and asked, "All right, well, may I go put the car in a space now?"

The trooper replied, "That would be a good idea, Miss Richman." Then he got into his own car and pulled away.

Lance commented coyly, "At least he knows your name, honey. That's worth something."

"Is it worth a hundred and fifty-five dollars?"

"You tell me."

Janice got behind the wheel and drove the Mercedes to the nearest empty space. When she walked back into the salon, she stopped still and stared open-mouthed at the back area. A man in a long monk's robe was standing next to the sink, staring back at her. His face was clean-shaven, revealing smooth skin and fine, angular features. His red hair was cut short, neatly layered, and parted on the left.

Ian gestured toward his customer with a flourish and said, "Everyone! Check out Encino Man."

Lance added, "Check him out indeed! Encino Man has evolved to Piltdown Man."

Ian asked, "What's that?"

"Don't you read our *National Geographic*s? I order them

especially for you. It's a better-looking cave man. A more modern one."

Janice approached Rowan, who was not moving a muscle. Slowly, she held out her hand and touched his hair, cautiously, as if he were a service dog. She whispered, "Mister Butler, you have been transformed."

Ian said, "Look at that hair color, Lance. And it isn't from a bottle."

Lance frowned.

Janice touched the coarse fiber of Rowan's sleeve and told him, "Now we need to buy you some clothes. Fast." She pointed at the door. "I saw a Ross Dress for Less right across the road."

Lance scoffed. "Do you want him to look like he shops at the Goodwill drop-off bin? No? Then we're going to Brooks Brothers. It's just two doors down."

"Brooks Brothers?"

"Yes! I was rocking their look late last year, around September/October. A Wall Street banker vibe—expensive suits, marvelous accessories, killer watches. The whole *greed-is-good* thing."

Lance led them on a brisk walk out the door and into the Brooks Brothers Outlet store. After a nod to an elderly clerk, he led Janice and Rowan to a back corner and assembled an outfit that included tan pants, a blue blazer, a yellow shirt, and a striped tie. He held up the ensemble and asked Janice, "You want to go full preppy, right? New York preppy, perhaps? Dalton to Choate to Yale?" When she did not reply immediately, he said, "No?" and switched out the shirt and tie for new ones. "How about this? Boston Latin to Andover to Harvard?"

Janice pointed to the second ensemble. She took the pants, blazer, and tie from Lance and handed them to Rowan, saying, "Here. Take these into the dressing room and put them on."

Rowan opened a wide wooden door and stepped into a narrow

room with metal wall hooks and a bench.

Lance inclined his head and whispered, "He walks funny, honey."

Janice conceded, "I know. It's like he's really thinking about it."

"What's there to think about?"

Janice shrugged. Lance held up a packaged yellow dress shirt to the clerk and asked, "All right if we open this?"

The man nodded and Lance removed the shirt, its cardboard stuffing, and a handful of pins. He shook it out, pronounced it, "Perfect," and handed it to Janice saying, "Here. Give this to Piltdown Man."

"To Mister Butler."

"That's what I meant."

Janice opened the dressing room door and shrieked. Rowan was standing there naked. She yanked it shut. "I'm so sorry!" After a moment, though, she leaned her face near the door and demanded to know, "Mister Butler, why aren't you wearing anything?"

"You said to put these on."

"Yes, but I didn't say to take off your underwear."

"I don't have underwear."

"No?"

"No. Monks wear robes."

Janice threw out her hands. "That's it?"

"Yes."

She turned to Lance. "Okay. I need underwear for him."

"What size?"

"I . . . I don't know."

"Well, how big was the package?"

Flustered, Janice answered, "What?"

"I'm teasing!"

Janice insisted, "That's not funny, Laurence. There is such a thing as a micro-phallus. Some men really do have them."

"Not men named Lance, honey." He snatched a three-pack of briefs down from a shelf. "Here. Hand him these."

"No! Can you do it? Please?"

Lance sighed. "Very well." He approached the dressing room door. "What's his name again?"

"Rowan Butler."

Lance turned the handle and opened the door six inches. "Rowan? These are for you, sweetie." Then he walked back to Janice, inclined his head, and whispered, "He is a small one, honey. You might want to throw him back."

"Stop that!"

"Perhaps he'll evolve to a homo erectus."

"Stop!"

"But the red hair is definitely real."

Janice laughed. "Yeah, well, that's more than you can say."

Lance hurried to a nearby shelf and pulled down a pair of brown leather shoes. "Oh wait! We *have* to get these. Look at the name."

Janice read aloud from the shoebox, "Plain Toe Monk Strap."

"Aren't they perfect?"

"No."

"But he's a monk!"

"Those shoes cost four hundred dollars."

"And why do we *not* care?"

Janice nodded nervously and muttered, "Okay. Okay."

Lance asked her, "By the way, sweetie, when we are done here, can I catch a ride into town with you? I'm meeting some people tonight. We'll be hanging ten, shooting the curl, and so on."

Janice looked doubtful. "I don't know. It'll be a tight fit in my car."

Lance replied, "Not for me! I'll sit up front." He added, "And you owe me. Remember? You begged for my help."

Janice agreed, "Okay. Okay."

"Oh, and can I *borrow* the car later tonight?"

"What?"

"Mine is in transition."

"Transition? From where?"

"It's in transition from *not* working to working. I never got the oil changed, or something, and it burned something up, so now they're replacing something. It's a huge mess."

Janice thought it over and replied, "Sure, Laurence. Sure. I really appreciate your help today."

He gently corrected her. "That's Lance."

Ten minutes later, Janice stood at the counter and pulled out MacDermott and Richman's American Express card. She clenched her teeth as the clerk rang up fifteen hundred dollars' worth of clothing, clothing already being worn by the transformed Rowan James Butler. When finished, Janice handed Rowan a blue shopping bag containing his monk's robe and sandals. Then she led her two companions out to her parking space.

As they approached the car, Lance called out, "Shotgun!"

Rowan asked, "What does that mean?"

Janice opened the door. She told Rowan, "Shotgun means you ride up front, next to the driver, like on the old stagecoaches of yore."

"The rider on a stagecoach would hold a shotgun?"

"Yes."

Rowan bent over and slid into the narrow seat in the back. He muttered to Janice, "Old things are already *of yore*. You would either say *old stagecoaches* or *stagecoaches of yore*, but not both."

She bugged out her eyes and muttered back, "Okay."

Lance added, "*Shotgun* is a cowboy term, Rowan. I went cowboy two years back. With memorable results."

As she started the engine, Janice's phone rang. She clicked it on and heard MacDermott's voice. "Richman! We have the LabTech results."

"Already?"

He growled, "It's a simple test. I can't believe what they charge for it."

"Well?"

"Well, the results are definitive. Your boy is Rowan James Butler, the sole heir to the Butlers' estate." Janice looked at Rowan in the rearview mirror as MacDermott concluded. "He is now a very wealthy man."

Janice pulled over at the corner of Seventh and Franklin Streets in Richmond. There were no parking spaces in front of the offices of MacDermott and Richman, so she suggested, "Why don't you hop out here, Mister Butler? You can wait for me right inside those glass doors."

He told her, "You should call me Rowan." Then he asked, "Where are you two going?"

Janice pressed the seat release and leaned forward to let him out. "I need to drop Laurence off at my apartment. Then I'll be right back." She had a second thought, "Or would you rather come along with us?"

Rowan said, "No. I'll get out here," and squeezed through the narrow space with his shopping bag.

Janice pointed at the building. "Go in and see Mister MacDermott. He's very anxious to meet you." She closed the door and pulled out, making a right turn, and quickly disappearing from view.

In no hurry to go inside, Rowan stepped back to the curb to take in the entire building. It was three stories high, and it extended a good forty yards from front to back. Unlike the modern office buildings around it, this one bore the architectural flourishes of a private home—clapboard siding, tall windows, two red brick chimneys rising up on either side.

He studied the windows of the two top floors. They were bare and dark, suggesting rooms that were no longer used. When he spotted a fire escape, he walked to it, set down the shopping bag, and jumped up three inches to touch the bottom-most rung. Then he craned his neck to follow the ladder's rise to the second and third floors, and on up to the roof.

Rowan wandered around the corner and stopped outside a narrow alcove. There he spotted a figure, partially hidden, just a few feet ahead of him. It was a man in dark blue coveralls, and he lay sleeping behind the Dumpster. Then he spotted a second man, inside the Dumpster itself. That one was wading hip-deep in the trash, selecting items, and dropping them into a supermarket shopping cart. The man's face and neck were badly sunburned. His gray, matted hair and scraggly beard stood out against his jacket, a black windbreaker with a *North Face* logo. The man turned around, met Rowan's gaze, and said, "What?"

Ten minutes later, when Janice walked up to the building, she saw Rowan and the *North Face* man standing by the front steps. Janice greeted Rowan with a wary nod. She said, "Is everything all right?"

Rowan told her, "Yes, but this man needs some money."

Janice looked the man up and down. She answered, "Yes, I'm sure he does."

"He has no place to stay, and he lost his job."

Janice took Rowan by the elbow and started him up the stairs, explaining, "He has several free shelters where he can stay." She added, "And he can get another job."

The scraggly man disagreed, "Not if you got a criminal record you can't."

Janice turned and addressed him directly. "That's not true. Basically, you can apply for and get *any* job that does not require a background check. And that's most jobs."

The man insisted, "That's not what I been told."

Janice let go of Rowan and turned out her palms. "By whom?"

"What?"

"Who told you that?"

The man shrugged and stammered a reply. "Some guy. A guy I talk to."

"Ah. Does this guy have a name?"

The man nodded and answered, "Yeah. Bruno."

"Well, you tell Bruno that he is wrong. And he should stop giving people bad legal advice."

The man scowled but could not formulate a reply. He turned away and stomped back toward the Dumpster.

Janice took hold of Rowan again and led him inside muttering, "He'll listen to a jailhouse lawyer, but not to a paralegal. That's how the poor stay poor." Janice paused in the reception area, pulled out her phone, and scrolled through her messages.

Rowan looked up at the ceiling. After a moment, he asked quietly, "What is that?"

Janice muttered absently, "What?"

"On the ceiling. Is that a painting?"

Janice put her phone away and looked. "Oh, *that*! That is a painting; yes; a mural."

Rowan twirled around slowly, taking in the images above him—a heavenly blue sky, shimmering white clouds, and a swirl of angelic creatures. He remarked, "It's beautiful."

"It is."

A man entered from the back area, stopped, and glared at Rowan. He was a powerfully built man in late middle age. He had a wide head and a round, compressed face, with dark eyes and a menacing five-o'clock shadow. His body seemed at odds with the clothes that hung from it, an impeccably tailored, navy-blue suit. He told Rowan, "You look just like her."

Rowan replied with curiosity, "Who?"

"Your mother."

Janice took a step forward and made a formal introduction. "Mister MacDermott, this is Rowan James Butler. Mister Butler, meet Mister MacDermott."

MacDermott nodded politely but kept his distance, offering no hand to shake. He said, "I saw you looking at that ceiling mural. Do you like that?"

Rowan answered, "Yes. Is it from the Sistine Chapel?"

"No. It's from the Palace of Versailles, so they tell me." He added, "That's in France." MacDermott pointed to Rowan's blue-and-gold shopping bag. "Are those your things?"

Rowan did not immediately reply, so Janice said, "Yes. That's all he has for now." She told Rowan, "I'll bring you some personal items tomorrow."

McDermott said, "Let's start with a bit of housekeeping. We're putting you in the old maids' quarters in the back. Missus MacDermott made up the bed in there, and it has an *en suite*." He paused, then defined the term. "It has its own bathroom. It'll do for tonight at least." MacDermott pulled his head back, as if appraising Rowan. He said, "You have her exact shade of red hair."

Rowan answered quietly, "Yes, well, that would make sense."

MacDermott swallowed. He took a moment to reflect, and then said, "Well, before we go any further, let me offer my condolences, Rowan, on the loss of your mother. And your father. They were both good friends of mine."

Rowan seemed surprised at the sentiment. He replied, "Oh. Thank you."

Janice added, "Yes! My condolences, too. I'm sorry I didn't . . . express those sooner. Things were so crazy today." No one said anything else until Janice pointed toward the back and suggested, "I'll show Rowan his room then."

MacDermott nodded sadly. "Yes. You do that, Richman. I'll see you in the morning." He added, "Rowan, can I get you anything before I leave?"

Rowan replied, "I would like something to read."

MacDermott gestured toward the bookcases in the meeting room. "I'm afraid we don't have much reading material here, unless you like law books."

Rowan told him, "I do."

MacDermott grinned. "Come on. Nobody likes law books."

Rowan shrugged and told him, "I'd at least like to read the legal papers that pertain to my own case."

"Oh? Well, sure."

"My parents' last will and testament perhaps? Do you have that? And any supporting materials?"

"I have all of those materials. They're written in legalese, though. You'll need our help interpreting them."

"I'll do my best."

MacDermott agreed reluctantly. "All right." He walked past Rowan to the front door, still offering no hand. He told Janice, "The Butlers' file is on top of my desk, next to the laptop."

"Yes, sir."

MacDermott nodded and pushed his way through the door. Janice gestured to Rowan to follow her. She led him down a corridor that had a large office on either side, one bearing a brass plaque for *Charles J. MacDermott, Jr.* and the other for *Mark Richman, Esq.*

She paused at MacDermott's door, telling Rowan, "Just a minute." She ducked in and came right back holding a brown expanding file. She held it out, saying, "Your bedtime reading material," and Rowan took it with his free hand.

At the end of the corridor, Janice unlocked and opened a door. She preceded Rowan into a small bedroom with Spartan furnishings—a single bed, a two-drawer dresser, and a rolling chair that matched the ones in the front office. She said, "Sorry it's so . . . sparse."

Rowan replied cheerfully, "It's far more than I'm used to."

"Oh?"

"Yes. *And* there's no one in here with me."

Janice asked, "What? Was someone in your room at the Community?"

"I didn't have a room. I slept on a cot in the residence hall, along with everyone else. Only Brother Abelard had his own room, and that was up by the main offices."

"What about Sister Agnes?"

"Sister Agnes was in the residence hall, too. They built a plywood wall near the far end, and her cot was behind that."

Janice said, "The Walls of Jericho, right?"

Rowan was confused. "The Walls of Jericho? Do you mean the Bible story?"

"No. It's an old movie, with Clark Gable."

"Oh." Rowan set his shopping bag and legal file on the bed.

Janice pulled open the door and pointed. "The bathroom is right here."

"Out in the corridor?"

"I'm afraid so."

Rowan looked toward MacDermott's office and asked, "So it's not *en suite*. Is it?"

She agreed, "No. It's not."

Rowan frowned. "People shouldn't use words if they don't know what they mean." He sat on the bed and bounced slightly, to test its firmness. Then he asked Janice, "Where will you be tonight? Back at your apartment?"

"Yes. It's close by. Just a few blocks."

"And what about Lance?"

"I'm not sure. He asked to borrow my car."

"Why?"

"To go out to a club. That may determine where he sleeps tonight."

Rowan seemed confused again. Janice clapped him lightly on the arm. "Don't worry about him. You have a good night. Enjoy some alone time. I'll come get you for breakfast tomorrow."

"What time?"

"Nine o'clock."

"All right."

Janice watched Rowan pick up the legal file and select a paper from it. She said, "Don't stay up too late, you know, reading." He didn't reply. She closed the door on him with the words, "And don't sleep in those clothes. They cost fifteen hundred dollars."

After two hours of reading, Rowan followed Janice's instructions and peeled off his new clothes. He lay back, naked, on the bed but soon sat back up. He leaned over the bed, dug his monk's robe out of the Brooks Brothers bag, and pulled it on. Then he began a night-time ritual that he had performed for years. Beginning at his left foot, and then progressing to his right foot, to his left hand, to his right hand, and to his neck, he clenched and unclenched each set of muscles, one time, for ten seconds. Then he returned to the left foot and did it all again. And then again, a third time through, clenching and unclenching his muscles until he fell, almost instantly, into a deep state of sleep.

After a few minutes, his eyes began to flutter behind his eyelids as a vivid dream filled his head. In the dream, he was floating above the St. Francis Community, over the main office and the residence hall. He studied every brown board; every gray line of stucco. He floated on, slowly, over a dilapidated wooden barn, and a corral with one recumbent, swayback horse. The dream ended at the far end of the campus, at the stone church, where Rowan hovered above a field of crumbling, weed-choked gravestones. Then he started to fall, as if to his own death. He found himself sitting up in a strange bed, in a strange room, awake and startled. After five minutes of hard breathing, he started his night-time ritual again.

Tuesday

Janice walked the three blocks from her apartment to the office building, arriving right at nine AM. She found Rowan standing outside clad once again in his full Brooks Brothers outfit.

He greeted her with, "Good morning, Janice. Where is Lance?"

"I don't know. He called me last night. He said he had to meet two guys."

Rowan replied, "Two guys?"

"Yeah. They were gonna go meet some more guys."

"More guys? Why?"

Janice asked him, "Seriously?" She started across the street. "Come on. I know a good place for breakfast."

"A restaurant?"

"Yes." She slowed to let Rowan fall in step with her. "When's the last time you were in a restaurant?"

"It's been a while. Years."

They approached a metal door emblazoned with the word *Luncheonette*. Janice held the door and let Rowan precede her inside. The breakfast rush had ended; only one couple sat at a long table directly in front of them. A smiling hostess, dressed in black, scooped up two menus and said, "You can sit anywhere you like."

Rowan nodded and took two measured steps forward. He pulled out a chair and started to sit with the lone dining couple, who looked at him curiously. Janice, puzzled at first, quickly took charge. "Rowan! It's, uh, it's not a family-style restaurant. If that's what you're thinking."

She slid her hand under his elbow, smiling in apology at the surprised couple, and led him to a table along the window.

The smiling hostess set down menus and asked, "Coffee?"

Janice said, "Yes, with cream."

Rowan told the hostess, "I'll have the same." He pointed to a picture on the menu. "And I'd like some scrambled eggs, bacon, and toast." He looked at Janice. "What about you?"

"That sounds fine. I don't do bacon, though." She added, "It's a Jew thing."

"Oh?" He told the hostess, "Then I won't, either."

The hostess retreated into the kitchen. After a moment, Janice cocked her head and smiled. "I must say: You look very presentable today, Rowan. You have a slight shadow of a beard, but only slight."

"Yes. I need to buy a razor. And I need to buy a toothbrush and a comb."

Janet held up one finger. She reached into her Michael Kors bag and pulled out a travel kit with a toothbrush, toothpaste, and floss. She said, "Here."

"You bought me these?"

"I had them in my apartment." Rowan took the kit and stared at it, puzzled. Janice explained, "You never know when you'll have a guest sleeping over. You need to be ready." She added, "It's another Jew thing."

"Well, I appreciate it."

They received their food within five minutes. A bearded, tattooed man from the kitchen plunked two large plates down on the table. Rowan stared at him silently until he left, then he asked Janice, "Are people with tattoos allowed to work in restaurants?"

She began eating immediately. "Sure. Why not?"

"Isn't it considered unsanitary?"

"No."

"Unappetizing?"

"Maybe. Maybe that's why they keep him in the back."

Rowan took his first bite. "Are tattoos common now?"

"Very common. You'll see them everywhere, on men and women both."

"Really? Women have them?"

"Some do." Janice assured him, "But I don't." Then she changed the subject. "Listen: I need to verify something."

Rowan answered agreeably. "All right. What?"

Janice pointed a pink fingernail at him. "You are Mister Rowan James Butler, are you not?"

Rowan smiled and replied, "I am."

"You are no longer—in any way, shape, or form—Brother Thomas."

He reflected on that for a moment, then answered. "No. I am not."

"You're sure? It's been very sudden."

"I am sure. I've been looking to leave Brother Thomas behind for awhile now."

Janice recalled, "It's funny; Brother Abelard tried to pass you off as someone named John Smith."

"Really?"

"Yes. He told me: *There are fifty thousand John Smiths in the United States.*"

Rowan shook his head; then he answered, "I believe the correct figure is seventeen thousand. There are actually more James Smiths and William Smiths than Johns."

Janice took a sip of her coffee. "Interesting. So . . . Tell me about your life out there."

"At the Community?"

"Yes."

"What do you want to know?"

"For openers, how long were you there?"

Rowan answered immediately, "Twenty years and two months."

"Wow. That's a long time."

"Is it?"

"It is to me. What did you do out there?"

"Do you mean, what was our day like?"

"Yes. Okay."

"We worked. We prayed. We had dinner. Then I read books." He added, "A book a night."

"Really? You read a whole book every night?"

"Yes. Sometimes two, if they were thin. Or simple-minded. The local library was very generous to the Community. Every week, Mister Cantwell would drive out and deliver a carton of books."

"Did the other monks read them, too?"

Rowan shook his head. "No. I don't think so."

"So this man brought the books especially for you?"

"I guess you could say that. Other people were welcome to read them, but they didn't."

Janice contemplated this while she took two more bites. Then she said, "Tell me about your parents."

Rowan shifted uncomfortably. He replied. "You probably know more about them than I do. At least over the past twenty years."

"I know what Mister MacDermott told me."

"What was that?"

"Well, your father was Doran Butler. Am I pronouncing it right?"

"Yes. The accent should be on *ran*."

"Is it Irish?"

"It's Celtic. It means *exiled one*."

"Your parents had large homes in Charleston and Savannah." She added, "They owned the law offices building in Richmond, too."

Rowan looked across the street. "Where I just slept."

"Yes."

"I read about that last night. In a summary document."

"Their money was mostly in real estate and stocks."

"I read a little about that, too."

Janice leaned closer and asked, "And you know that Doran had a first wife. Right?"

"Of course."

"Named Katherine?"

"Yes."

She grimaced. "And they had two children—Kaitlyn, a-k-a *Kitty*, and Ewell." She turned the grimace into a silly smile. "A-k-a *Ewell*."

Rowan frowned. "I remember them. Are they coming today?"

Janice leaned back. "Oh yes. Most definitely. They have been driving my dad crazy, as you might imagine."

"Why?"

Janice answered carefully, "Dad may have . . . led them to believe that you were . . . gone." Rowan cocked his head at the word *gone*, so she went on. "If not dead, then lost somehow. Wandering around talking to yourself. Homeless."

Rowan repeated the word, "Homeless," and then added, "I have met many homeless people. They would wander into the Community."

"Yeah? All the way out there? What would you do with them?"

"We'd feed them, and clothe them, and they'd go on their way. Some were mentally ill."

Janice agreed. "Oh yes."

"A few were veterans; veterans of wars."

"Right. With PTSD."

Janice was about to translate the acronym, but Rowan beat her to it. "Post-Traumatic Stress Disorder."

She replied, "Right."

"And some, I'd say, were just plain unlucky."

Janice disagreed. "Or just plain lazy."

Rowan pulled back and looked at her. He fell quiet for a moment. Then he asked, "What do you know about my mother?"

"I know what I read at the office. And what I heard there."

Rowan stated, "Her name was Siobhan."

"Oh? Is that how you pronounce it?"

"Yes. It's Irish, too: *shi-vonn*." He paused and added, "Kind of like *chiffon*."

"Siobhan Marie Kelly?"

"Yes. She was from Savannah."

Janice pointed out, "Like me."

Rowan stared at Janice expectantly. "Yes. What else can you tell me about her?"

Janice took in a fork-full of eggs and swallowed. "Well, let's see. I know where she met your father."

Janice paused and waited him out, forcing him to ask, "Okay. Where?"

"Right where you slept last night."

"The office building?"

"Yes. Mister MacDermott introduced them to each other. Do you want to hear the official version of that? Or do you want to hear the gossip?"

Rowan answered warily, "I suppose the truth lies somewhere between the two?"

"Yes. Well, according to my dad, Doran Butler, despite being rather diminutive, and totally bald, was a real ladies' man. He made no pretense of being faithful to his first wife."

Rowan asked, "Your father said that about him?"

"Yes."

"He called my father a bounder?"

"What?"

"A roué?"

"I remember him using the term *a lying sack of shit*. But when your father met Siobhan Kelly, he changed; he became totally smitten. Apparently, *she* was different from all the others."

"Smitten? Like *smite*? Like to strike a blow?"

"Yes, I suppose so. Well, in pretty short order, Siobhan became Doran's mistress, and then she became pregnant, and then all hell broke loose. Katherine found out about the affair and threatened to sue for divorce. Doran said he didn't care; that she should sue, because he was leaving her and the children anyway."

Rowan nodded rapidly; he indicated she should continue.

"According to my dad, Katherine engaged a powerhouse legal firm from Atlanta who completely steamrolled Mister MacDermott. Doran lost everything to Katherine, but he didn't care. He simply started over again, building a new business, and a new fortune, with a new wife."

"Wife? They were married then?"

"Yes, they were—about six months after you were born; one week after Katherine died in an auto accident. Doran, despite his philandering ways, was a staunch Catholic. He waited until his first wife was dead to marry his second."

"And that's what made me a bastard?"

"Technically, yes. You were born out of wedlock. But then you were legitimized by their marriage."

"Legitimized in whose eyes?"

"Pardon me."

"God's? The Pope's? The Archbishop of Canterbury's?"

"I wouldn't know about them."

"In the siblings' eyes?"

"I doubt that very much."

Rowan looked out the window at the law offices. He said, "I have a vague recollection of Kitty and Ewell. Of one Thanksgiving Day."

"Really? You celebrated Thanksgiving together?"

"Just once. When I was little. Six years old or so. My mother tried to mend fences with a family dinner, but it didn't work out." He looked at Janice. "I remember sitting at a children's table, and Kitty pointing to me and saying, *We need a bastard's table for him.* I didn't know what she meant."

"That was nasty."

"The whole dinner was nasty. My mother got very upset, and asked them to leave, and we never did anything like that again."

Janice tapped a fingernail on the table and told him, "Well, be prepared today. Kitty hasn't changed. She and Ewell want to get their hands on Doran Butler's money. I should say, on the rest of his money. They were set for life with Katherine's divorce settlement, but they think they are entitled to more; to all of it. As it is structured now, it could all go to you." Janice paused, then asked, "And do you know how much there is?"

"I do. I read the will."

"You really did? The whole thing?"

"Yes. It was poorly written, but the list of assets was clear enough. It's a substantial fortune."

"It is." Janice took a sip of coffee. "My dad says Kitty and Ewell won't rest until they get their grubby hands on it."

Rowan took the last sip of his coffee. "I haven't seen Kitty or Ewell since that Thanksgiving dinner. I haven't even thought about them."

"Well, they've been thinking about you, at least since yesterday afternoon."

Rowan placed his hands on the table and spread them apart. "We were related, I suppose, but we lived *unrelated* lives. We walked down different paths. We went to different summer camps. We attended different boarding schools."

"Good boarding schools, I expect."

"I'm sure they were. They weren't good for me, though."

"No?"

"No. I was constantly getting poor grades, but . . . " His voice trailed off.

Janice prompted him gently, "But what?"

"But I felt, inside, that I was really smart; maybe smarter than anyone there."

The hostess arrived with their check. Janice handed her a credit card, and she took it away. Then Rowan asked, "So how did my parents' story end?"

"What do you mean?"

"How did Doran and Siobhan die?"

"Oh." Janice inhaled deeply, closed her eyes, and exhaled. She told him, "They died in an accident involving a drunk driver." She added, " Unfortunately, the drunk driver was Doran. Mister MacDermott had fought several DUI cases for your father before. He had just gotten his license restored when the fatal crash happened."

"Where did it happen?"

"On a bridge between Georgia and South Carolina. Right on the state line, and I mean exactly on the line. That complicated the case. There was an accusation from the South Carolina side that the Georgia state troopers actually pushed the car five feet forward, fully into South Carolina, and then called it a day."

The hostess returned with the credit card. Janice totaled the bill, then said, "Let's resume this discussion later, because I think it's important. Okay?"

Rowan agreed, "Sure."

Janice stood. "We should get over to the meeting room."

Rowan got up and followed Janice out the door and across the now-busy street. They climbed the steps of the law offices and entered the outer room. Rowan pointed to the empty desk and chair and asked, "Is there usually a secretary here?"

Janice said, "Sort of. Missus MacDermott comes in most afternoons and does typing and filing."

"The boss's wife?"

"Yeah. Pretty ghetto, huh?" She lowered her voice. "Honestly? How well can a firm be doing if the boss's wife is working there?" She added, "And if Kitty and Ewell Butler are their top clients?"

Rowan took in this information, then replied, "So the firm—that is, Charles J. MacDermott, Junior, and Mark Richman, Esquire—want to keep Kitty and Ewell happy?"

Janice laughed mirthlessly. "Yeah. Good luck with that. Right?"

Just then, MacDermott entered from the back corridor carrying the brown expanding file in one hand and a large laptop in the other. He nodded briefly at Rowan and Janice and preceded them into a wood-paneled meeting room. He set the file and laptop down on a highly polished table ringed by six black leather chairs. MacDermott claimed the seat at the head of the table, opened the laptop, and grumbled, "I forget the goddamn password."

Janice walked to the far side of the table and took the seat next to her boss. She indicated that Rowan should sit next to her. Then she told MacDermott, "The password is: *M-and-R,* all one word, followed by *one two three four*."

MacDermott typed that in, nodded, and closed the lid. He looked up and addressed Rowan formally. "As you know, Rowan, this firm has represented your father, and then your father and your mother, for over thirty years. Upon their demise, therefore, we undertook to execute their last will and testament. You are named as the heir in that document. Therefore, we made an initial attempt to locate you, but we could not. My partner Mark Richman was in charge of that effort."

He stole a quick look at Janice. "Frankly, I was not sure how hard he was trying. We certainly did *not* locate you in time for your parents' funeral, and for that I apologize. Anyway, we brought in Janice here, and she managed to find you in time for the reading of the will." He smiled at Janice. "Sometimes you have to go the extra mile. Go out there and do what it takes to get the job done. Right, Richman?"

Janice muttered, "Yes, sir."

He winked at Rowan, "Sometimes you have to bend the rules a little, you know?"

Rowan considered his words; then admitted, "No. I don't know."

MacDermott turned up his palms. He explained, "You have to do what you have to do, Rowan. You have to be willing to get your hands dirty. You have to work with, let's call them, *less-than-reputable* people sometimes in order to defend a client. In your case, though, our own, very reputable little Janice here managed to go out and get the job done."

MacDermott turned back to Janice and asked, cavalierly, "Where's your salon friend? Is he dressing somebody?" He winked at Rowan again. "Or undressing somebody maybe?"

Janice answered, "Laurence went out partying last night. I expect he is somewhere sleeping it off today. I hope it's not in my car."

MacDermott turned serious. He asked her, "And what about your father?"

Janice tensed. "What about him?"

"Is he sleeping it off somewhere, too?"

"I don't know, Mister MacDermott."

"I don't know, either. Guess who else doesn't know: your father. He claims to have blackouts now. He can't remember where he's been or what he's done. At least that's what he tells me."

Janice whispered, "I didn't know about that."

"Yes. Well, you need to. He's definitely getting worse."

The three sat in awkward silence for thirty seconds until MacDermott attempted to lighten the mood. He smiled at Rowan and told him, "You clean up good! What a makeover!"

Rowan said, "Yeah. Lance did a good job."

"Who's Lance?"

"That's Laurence," Rowan explained. "That's what he asked to be called."

"Lance huh? And he owns the salon?"

"Yes."

MacDermott chuckled. "Janice told me about some of the wisecracks they were making there." When Rowan did not react, he looked at Janice and provided examples: "Calling you a cave man. What else? Encino Man? Piltdown Man?"

Rowan muttered, "That was stupid."

MacDermott said, "What's that?"

Rowan replied firmly, "Those remarks. They were stupid. *Encino Man* wasn't a real cave man. It was a made-up movie."

MacDermott replied evenly, "Okay."

"Piltdown Man was not real, either. It was a scientific hoax that tarnished the reputation of the great Jesuit anthropologist Teilhard de Chardin. He lent his prestige to the Piltdown Man claim, and he paid a terrible price for it."

"You don't say."

Rowan continued, "The same thing happened to the British historian Hugh Trevor-Roper. He lent his name and prestige to a claim that the diaries of Adolf Hitler had been found. Turns out they were a hoax. We don't recall the names of the hoaxers; just of the distinguished historian who lost his good name because of them."

All MacDermott could manage was another, half-hearted, "You don't say."

Rowan locked eyes with him and said, "When I *don't say* something, Mister MacDermott, you will know it because there will be no words coming out of my mouth."

The lawyer opened his own mouth to reply but thought better of it.

After another awkward silence, Rowan pointed to the camera mounted on the far wall of the office. "Is that a movie camera?"

MacDermott started to laugh, but then adjusted and answered seriously, "Well, sort of. It's part of a security system that records what we say and do."

"Oh? Why is that?"

"So we can have a record, in case we need it. The camera has a time stamp, so its recordings are useful as evidence."

Rowan studied the camera until the sound of an opening door drew everyone's attention to the outer office. Janice announced, with relief, "Ah! Here they are."

A woman and man entered through the glass doors, turned right, and walked briskly into the meeting room. Both cast wary glances at Rowan. The woman had lacquered blonde hair, sharp facial features, and a wiry athletic body. The man was taller, and heavier, with thinning brown hair and rounded shoulders. They pulled out chairs across from Rowan and sat without a word.

A short, well-dressed man entered right behind them. He had a trim build and a handsome face, except for a pair of watery, blood-shot eyes. He pulled out the chair across from Janice and sat. Janice spoke to him softly, "Good morning, Dad."

He did not reply.

MacDermott wasted no time in opening the meeting. He said, "All right. Everybody's here. I don't believe you three have seen each other in years, so let me make introductions." He turned to Rowan and said, "This is Miss Kitty Butler; next to her is Mister Ewell Butler." MacDermott turned to the siblings. "And this is Mister Rowan James Butler."

Kitty studied Rowan briefly and commented, "No way." MacDermott pulled a report from his file and offered it to Kitty. She asked him, "What is that?"

MacDermott explained, "It's the report from LabTech; the DNA report. The one I emailed you about. His hair samples conclude—"

Kitty snapped, "Hair samples, my ass," so MacDermott lowered the report.

When she said nothing further, MacDermott cleared his throat and moved on. "All right. We are here to execute the last will and testament of my late clients, Missus Siobhan Kelly Butler and Mister Doran Michael Butler."

Upon hearing her father's name, Kitty turned to her brother and snarled, "Doran, yeah. *Doran ran.* That's what Mom liked to say."

Ewell confirmed, "She said that a lot."

"And *Lemon Chiffon.* That's what she called his little whore. Lemon Chiffon Kelly." Kitty looked at Rowan. "Doran was married to *our* mother, you know. Ewell and I were both born within the bonds of holy matrimony. Within the Holy Catholic Church. You were not. Do you know what that makes you?" Ewell opened his mouth to interrupt; perhaps to head his sister off, but he could not. She declared, "A bastard. A dirty little bastard."

Mark Richman spoke up. "Let's keep this civil, Kitty."

Kitty turned to him. "Fine. Yeah. Let's get this shit over with."

Mark Richman reached forward and took hold of the laptop. The group watched him in silence as he clicked on an icon and adjusted the volume. Then they heard a new voice ask, "Are you ready for me now?"

Mark Richman replied, "Yes, doctor. Thank you for making yourself available today at such short notice." He turned the screen around until Rowan and Janice were staring at the face of a bald, bespectacled man. The man leaned back in his seat, revealing a tan suit and tie and a wall arrayed with diplomas.

Mark Richman, by way of introduction, explained, "This is Doctor Walter Bresnahan from Virginia Commonwealth University."

Janice, clearly confused, asked, "A doctor?"

Her father explained further, "He is a doctor of psychiatry at the VCU Medical Center. My clients, Kitty and Ewell Butler, have requested that Doctor Bresnahan conduct a mental competency test on the man recently identified as Rowan James Butler."

Janice was appalled. "No way! You can't be springing this on us."

Kitty snapped at her, "Oh, shut up, Wonder Girl."

To which Janice hissed, "You shut up."

Mark Richman looked pained. He held up a shaky hand and told his daughter, "Kitty and Ewell are my clients, Janice." He pointed to Rowan, "He is not." He tilted the laptop and spoke to it, "Please explain our concerns, Doctor, about Mister Rowan James Butler."

Mark Richman set the laptop back down, and the psychiatrist took over. "Certainly. I have read the profile on Mister Butler, and I am concerned about his history of mental health issues." The doctor turned several pages of a report that lay before him and continued. "Issues such as recurring and debilitating behaviors, Obsessive Compulsive behaviors, which he displayed as a child. These have been recorded and reported by a series of teachers in a series of very reputable private schools." He looked up, "And, most alarmingly of all, the issue of an acute psychotic episode he suffered, at the age of nineteen, as reported by the Dean of Appomattox College."

He explained to the group, "It is not uncommon for mental health issues to emerge in a man's late teens or early twenties, and it often happens in college due to the pressure to get good grades. Apparently, this is what happened to Mister Butler."

Janice spoke up. "How long ago was that? Twenty years?" to which Kitty replied, "Shut the hell up. Let the doctor talk."

MacDermott intervened. "So, Doctor, how can we put everyone's fears to rest about Mister Butler's mental competence?"

The doctor replied, "I would like to ask him some simple questions. His answers should provide us with a starting point for an evaluation."

Janice held up both hands, in a *stop* gesture, and announced, "No way."

MacDermott started to agree with her, but Rowan interrupted, "I have no objection to that."

After exchanging a worried glance, both Janice and her boss sat back to let the evaluation proceed.

Rowan leaned closer to the laptop, prompting the doctor to begin. "Mister Butler, can you tell me the name of the current President of the United States?"

"Certainly."

After a pause, in which it became clear that Rowan was not going to elaborate, the doctor prompted him, "Well, what is that name?"

"Donald Trump."

"All right. And can you tell me who was the previous President of the United States?"

"Barack Obama."

"Good. Now—"

Rowan suddenly challenged him, "Is this the standard for mental competency, Doctor? Knowing the presidents of the United States?"

"Yes, in part."

"Very well, then. Here goes. The first five Presidents were: George Washington, John Adams, Thomas Jefferson, James Madison, and James Monroe. Parenthetically, they were all Virginians except for Adams. The sixth president, John Quincy Adams, was the son of that one non-Virginian. He was followed by Andrew Jackson, Martin Van Buren, and William Henry Harrison."

Kitty said, "Enough with the names! He's acting like this is a big joke."

Ewell agreed, "This is ridiculous."

But Rowan was not finished. "Harrison was followed by John Tyler who, to this day, remains the *last* Virginian ever elected to the office. Isn't that remarkable? Five of the first ten, and then none thereafter?"

MacDermott put an end to the discussion by extending his arms and announcing, "I believe we can concede Mister Butler's knowledge on that question."

Rowan extended his own arms, protesting, "But I'm not finished. There are thirty-five more to go." He looked around the room and suggested, "Let's do them together. *Or* we could alternate." He asked the psychiatrist, "Who is next, Doctor?" and received no answer. "Who is next, Law Offices of MacDermott and Richman? Who is next, half-siblings?" He concluded, "Apparently, I am the only one in this room who is mentally competent."

Kitty muttered to Ewell, "Maybe he's some kind of smart idiot, like *Rain Man*."

Ewell turned to Mark Richman. "You told us he was non compost mentis."

Rowan corrected his half-brother: "That's non *compos* mentis."

"What?"

"It's *compos;* not *compost*."

Kitty backhanded her brother's arm. "Can we stop with the Pig Latin?"

Ewell groused, "It's not Pig Latin."

Rowan added, "It means *not in control of mind*."

Ewell replied, "I know what it means. I attended law school." He looked at Mark Richman for confirmation, and received a slight head nod in return. Ewell added, "Until I caught mono."

Kitty glared at Mark Richman. "This . . . This total stranger, some guy that your kid found wandering in the woods, just shows up and tries to steal a third of our estate? Are you kidding me?"

Ewell looked askance at his sister while MacDermott shifted in his chair. It was MacDermott who spoke up. "You really should read my emails, Kitty. The fact is, Rowan James Butler is entitled to his parents' *entire* estate."

Kitty's stunned silence froze them all in place; then she found her voice. She screeched at Mark Richman, causing him to wince. "You promised *us* that money!"

Mark Richman swallowed and answered calmly, "I didn't promise anything, Kitty. I said that if the primary heir was not available, the money would be yours, pending investigation."

Kitty's rage turned to Janice. "Yes! Investigation by Wonder Girl here! She found this . . . bastard out in some shitville somewhere, and now he's the heir to all my family's money? Are you fucking kidding me?"

MacDermott held up a document, and read from it. "According to the will, as the only child of Doran and Siobhan Butler, Rowan is the primary heir to their estate. You and Ewell are the collateral heirs to the estate, collecting only if Rowan was deceased or could not be located. It's the way the will is structured, Kitty. Don't blame us."

Mark Richman, through closed eyes, elaborated. "The detective agency's report stated that Rowan James Butler enrolled in Appomattox College, failed to complete any courses, had a psychotic episode, and then disappeared. For twenty years. We were prepared to conclude from this research that he had either died or become insane; that he had indeed become *non compos mentis*."

Kitty warned him, "Don't start that shit again."

MacDermott said, "We searched for Rowan James Butler without success. But then, Janice had a hunch."

MacDermott looked at Janice, prompting her to pick up the narrative. "I located Appomattox College on Google maps. I clicked on the satellite view. I looked for places that a young man could walk to from the college."

Kitty said, "Wonderful! Save it for someone who gives a shit." She stood up, leveled a finger at Mark Richman, and warned him "If you let this . . . nut-job walk away with our money, I will fucking destroy you!"

Kitty turned and tried to leave, but she was unable to. She looked down at her right shoe. The pointy heel had wedged between two floorboards and was now stuck. She grabbed her own knee and pulled up forcefully. The shoe broke off at the heel. Kitty planted her bare right foot and kicked off the left one, bouncing it off Mark Richman's leg. She snarled, "These are goddamn Jimmy Choos! They're not supposed to fall apart!"

Ewell picked up the shoe and offered it to her, but she snapped, "No! The hell with them! I'm throwing them out. Let's go!" She stomped out of the office in her bare feet, not even turning to deliver her final words to Rowan's face, "This isn't over, Rain Man! You had better watch your back!"

Ewell followed, admonishing her in a low voice, "Kitty! Don't threaten someone out loud, in front of witnesses. It's illegal."

Mark Richman picked up the left shoe, squinted at it, and remarked, "It's true. These are Jimmy Choos, Janice. Do you want them?"

Janice shook her head. "No." She added, "Gross."

"Okay. I'll put them in the Goodwill box."

She said, "No again, Dad! No designer shoes for the homeless. Some bag lady will break her ankle in those heels. Just throw them in the trash."

MacDermott told his partner, "I'd say we're through with that psychiatrist."

Mark Richman tipped the laptop, muttered, "Thank you, Doctor Bresnahan," and unceremoniously shut the lid. Then he rose and followed his clients out the front door.

MacDermott sighed. "All right. That part is over and done. At least I hope so. Let us now proceed to the more pleasant part—to the allocation of assets." He turned over several pages, then told Rowan, "You inherit Doran Butler's stock portfolio, showing a current value in excess of ten million dollars. You also inherit three high-value properties that were held in your mother's name."

MacDermott produced three pieces of paper and spread them on the table so that Rowan could see. Each had a Kodachrome picture stapled to it showing a building. He said, "The first property is in Richmond, Virginia. In fact, it is right here, where we currently sit. Seven-o-seven East Franklin Street. It is a large private home that has been converted to commercial office space in accordance with local zoning laws.

"The second property is in Charleston, South Carolina." He looked at Rowan and added, "That is approximately a six-hour drive from here. The property is located at Church and South Battery Streets, facing White Point Garden.

"The third property is in Savannah, Georgia, which is another two hours further south. The Butlers maintained a house there in Madison Square, at Bull and East Charlton Streets."

MacDermott concluded, "All of these properties are managed, of course, by the firm of MacDermott and Richman. As are all of the stocks."

Rowan rearranged the papers before him. He studied the Kodachrome images intensely, fully engrossed, as if he were unaware of anyone else in the room. He lowered his head, closed his eyes, and pressed his fingers against his eyelids.

After a full minute of watching him, Janice asked, "What are you thinking, Rowan?"

He looked up at her slowly and replied. "I am thinking of a scripture. From the New Testament."

"From the Bible?"

"Yes. The Book of John, Chapter Fourteen, Verse Two: *In my Father's house are many mansions. I go to prepare a place for you.*"

MacDermott rolled his eyes at Janice. He said, "Well, be that as it may, Rowan, we'll do what we can to help you make informed decisions about these properties. As part of our service, Janice will drive you to see the other two *mansions* in the next two days. They are very valuable properties, and the real estate market is up in both cities, so it's the perfect time to sell."

Rowan pointed to the photos. "Sell? Why would I sell these?"

MacDermott assured him, "You'll see. They are quite large; they *are* mansions, as you said. A single man such as yourself, a simple-living man, a recently monastic-living man, would have no use for *one* mansion, let alone two."

MacDermott pointed to the office walls. "We also have to count this building. So make that *three* mansions for just one man." He paused to do a mental calculation. "Three mansions with a combined living area of over thirty-thousand square feet."

Rowan mulled that figure and said, "I just met a man who lived out of a shopping cart. I'd say it measured about two feet by three feet. So his equivalent living area would be six square feet?"

MacDermott replied tentatively, "I suppose."

Rowan went on, "That would be one-fifth of one percent of mine? Point zero-zero-zero-two of my living area?"

MacDermott shook his head. "That's one way of looking at it." He looked at Janice again, then added, "I realize that this has all come as a great shock to you, Rowan."

Rowan glanced down at the papers. "Not really. No." He added, "I knew most of this."

"How?"

"I read it in the will last night."

MacDermott's face showed surprise. "Really? You read the whole thing?"

"Yes."

MacDermott grinned at Janice. "Hell, even I didn't do that." He turned back to Rowan. "I assume you will want us to keep managing your assets, to keep them growing."

Rowan scooped up the three papers. He replied, "No. You should not assume that."

MacDermott blinked and said, "Pardon me?"

Rowan stood and told him, "I said: You should not assume that. I'll make a decision about them by the end of the week."

Janice rose, too.

MacDermott remained in his seat, frowning deeply, as Janice followed Rowan into the entrance area. Once they were beyond her boss's hearing, she told him, "I'm sorry about that psychiatrist thing. I didn't know it was going to happen. That wasn't right."

"No need to be sorry. I didn't mind."

"That was really cool what you did."

"What?"

"That presidents thing. You turned the tables on them."

"Oh, that. That was just a parlor trick." He turned back and looked into the meeting room. "I didn't want the people in there to think I was stupid."

"Well, you succeeded in that!"

"People have always assumed I was stupid. I used to let them think it, but—" his voice trailed off— "but not anymore."

"Well, no, you shouldn't. Especially not with people like Kitty and Ewell."

Rowan shrugged. He said, "Kitty and Ewell are still children; still sitting at the children's table at Thanksgiving dinner. I wouldn't take them too seriously."

"You had *better* take them seriously! She just threatened you!"

Rowan shrugged. Janice leaned forward and stared out onto the street. A *Virginia State Police* car, the same one as the day before, was now sitting at the curb. And the same state trooper was standing beside it, apparently waiting for them to come out.

Rowan opened the door and held it for Janice. She gave the state trooper a brief, compact wave and asked, "What's going on?"

The trooper raised his sunglasses before answering. "Miss Richman. It's Dan Bateman. From yesterday. State Trooper Bateman? Do you remember me?"

"I do. You gave me a ticket."

"Yes."

"And I asked if you were Jewish."

"Yes." He answered, "Well, I'm half-Jewish." He opened the passenger side door and told her, "I need you to come with me, Miss Richman."

"Why? Is something wrong?"

"I'm afraid so. Please come with me. I need you to identify your car and to provide a statement."

"Come with you where?"

"To the crime scene. It's about a ten-minute drive."

Janice turned to Rowan with a puzzled look. She muttered, "Crime scene?"

Rowan answered with enthusiasm, "Let's go."

Janice asked the trooper, "Can my client come with us?"

"Does he know anything about your car? Or its driver?"

Janice replied, "About Laurence? Is that who you mean? Laurence Myers?"

"Yes, Miss."

"He does. He knows about Laurence, and my car and . . . what? Did Laurence do something to my car?"

The trooper did not answer the question. Instead, he told Rowan, "You can sit in the back, sir." He explained to Janice, "It's best if we do our talking at the crime scene."

He closed the car door on Janice's words as she repeated, "The crime scene?"

Rowan took his place in the back and buckled his seat belt. Trooper Bateman pulled away quickly, and the three drove in silence. Janice tried not to imagine what Laurence, perhaps inebriated, might have done to her car. After a short drive north they turned a corner and Janice gasped audibly.

A half dozen police cars with flashing lights had formed a perimeter around a green stucco building. Atop the building, a neon sign displayed the words: *The Virginia Squire* in red cursive letters. Two *City of Richmond Police* cars were blocking the entrance to the parking lot.

Trooper Bateman pulled next to the nearest police car and held up a copper badge. The driver acknowledged it with a nod and then backed up, allowing Trooper Bateman to drive into the lot. There was only one car parked in there, and Janice gasped again when she saw it. The blue Mercedes, with the red clay undercarriage, sat there on four flattened tires. The passenger side and part of the back were pockmarked with bullet holes; so was a nearby section of the green stucco wall.

Trooper Bateman rolled to a stop behind the Mercedes and turned to Janice. "Laurence Myers was the man who tried to bribe me yesterday, right?"

Janice gulped and answered, "He was. Yes. He was the guy at the salon."

"Well, I am sorry to tell you, Miss Richman, but Mister Myers is dead."

"What?"

"He was apparently murdered, right here, in your car, last night."

"No!" Janice sputtered, "No! Who? Who would do that?"

The trooper answered kindly, "The police know very little at this point, Miss. They're waiting for forensics to arrive. They called me because your license plate showed up on their computers. From yesterday."

"What? How?"

"From the ticket."

Janice inhaled and exhaled rapidly. She fanned her face with her right hand. She asked, "What about Laurence's parents? Do they know?"

The trooper replied, "No. We have not yet notified next of kin."

Janice told him, "They live in Savannah."

The trooper nodded; he suggested, "Would you like to call them?"

"No!"

"All right. Sorry."

After a respectful pause, Rowan asked the trooper, "Is it all right if I get out of the car?"

"You're free to get out, sir. Just don't get in the officers' way. And don't touch anything."

Rowan exited the back seat and stepped carefully to a spot three feet from the blue Mercedes. He studied the grisly scene in great detail; then he heard footsteps coming up behind. Janice and Trooper Bateman took up positions on either side of him.

When Janice spotted the trail of blood spilling down the car's back bumper, she gasped again. Her eyes followed the dark red trail down to a coagulated puddle on the blacktop. Her mouth opened wide in horror, and all color seemed to drain from her face. She lurched off to the right, clutching her midsection as if she had been spitted, and Trooper Bateman followed. Then she bent forward and projectile vomited, scattering pieces of egg and toast across the asphalt.

Officer Bateman stood one step back, with his right hand extended, as if wondering if he should touch her. He retracted his hand and waited until Janice righted herself, turned to him, and whispered, "Who could do such a thing to Laurence?"

Trooper Bateman looked around and replied, "Well, this is a high-crime area. We figure he met the wrong person, or persons, out here in the parking lot. Most likely for a drug buy. And they just opened up on him."

Rowan turned toward them and said, "He carried a lot of cash; a roll of hundred dollar bills."

The trooper pulled out a notebook and jotted down this information, muttering, "That's right. I saw some of those."

But Janice shook her head. She answered adamantly, "No! Laurence never took drugs. He was *very* opposed to them." The trooper raised his shoulders up and down. Janice turned her back on the bloody scene and asked, "What happens to my car?"

"It will be impounded as evidence." He looked at her, "I assume you have insurance."

She answered, "Yes. Of course."

"Insurance will likely pay for a car rental." He continued, "Do you have gap insurance?"

"I don't know."

"If you do, and this is totaled, they will buy you a new model of the same car."

Janice mumbled, "I see."

The trooper led Janice and Rowan back to his patrol car. He said, "I'll drop you off where I found you. Okay?"

Janice turned and took a last look back at her car, and at the pockmarked green wall. She shuddered and nodded affirmatively.

After they had maneuvered back through the police cars, and were driving south, Rowan leaned forward and asked Trooper Bateman, "So what comes next? What is your process for finding the killer?"

The trooper answered, "Our process? What do you mean? What steps do we take?"

"Yes."

"Well, I mentioned before that the forensics people were on their way."

"Yes. Why weren't they on the scene already?"

"I don't know. They get busy sometimes. Like anybody else."

"Like during rush season?"

The trooper looked at him in the rearview mirror. "What?"

"At the Community, we had a rush season. It was right before the holiday season. Are there rush seasons in police work?"

Trooper Bateman answered, "Sure. Some times are busier than others. Like during the holidays."

"You, too?"

"Yes."

Rowan said, "Then it's all hands on deck?"

"It sure is."

Janice finally spoke. "I just texted Allstate. They told me that I *do* have gap insurance."

The trooper said, "That's good."

"I didn't even know it. And they said to go ahead and rent a car."

Janice turned her attention to her phone, and Rowan resumed his questioning. "So, the forensics people gather the evidence—like fingerprints and blood—and what else?"

Trooper Bateman added, "Footprints, hairs, threads from clothing."

"Okay. Then does that body of evidence become the sourcebook for the authorities, like the Bible of the case? Must everything derive from that one, true source? Or can you take a wider, more holistic approach?"

The trooper looked in the mirror again. He grimaced and answered, "I wouldn't call it *holistic*. That sounds a little New Age, like Rolfing; a little too flakey for police work." He went on. "We'd never do something weird like call in a psychic, if that's what you mean."

"A psychic? Are there really such people?"

"Let's say there are people who claim to be. They contact us and say things like: *I had a vision of this crime. I saw exactly what happened.*"

"And what do you say back?"

"We say: *Uh, no, you didn't.*"

After a pause, Rowan said, "We had a monk back at the Community who had a psychic vision."

The trooper raised his eyebrows.

Rowan continued. "He was called Brother Victor. He was very old, and very foreign. He never said where he came from, but I inferred that it was from Eastern Europe.”

Trooper Bateman asked, “Why?”

“He used the word *Cossacks* frequently. And he talked about rhythmic gymnastics.”

“And that means he was from Eastern Europe?”

“That was my inference. That he was from one of the former Soviet Bloc countries.”

“Okay.”

“So, one morning after Matins—” Rowan paused to define that as, “our morning prayers—he asked Brother Abelard for permission to speak to the group. The abbot granted permission, and Brother Victor rose and stood before us, very agitated, and declared, *I have had a psychic vision!*”

Trooper Bateman commented, “Uh oh. Here we go.”

“*I have had a vision! I have seen a hanging man!*” Rowan paused; then continued, “We all stared at him, waiting for more, but that was it. He stopped talking and walked out of the church, so we did, too, just like we would on any other day.

“We all arrived at the back door to the bakery. Brother Abelard went to insert his key in the door, but he pulled back, surprised to see that the door was not locked. He pushed the door open and led the way in. Then he let out a sound, a deep, anguished sound. We all packed in behind him and saw what he saw: Another monk, a troubled fellow known as Brother Paul, was hanging from a high, black steam pipe with a rope around his neck. His face had turned an inhuman shade of purple, like a rotten eggplant.

“Brother Abelard dispatched two monks to find a ladder and a carving knife. They cut Brother Paul down and set him on the bakery floor. Brother Abelard then summoned the police, and an ambulance, but Brother Paul was long past saving. The paramedics opined that he had been dead for several hours.”

Rowan stopped speaking. After a moment, Trooper Bateman said, “Are you telling us that this Brother Victor had a vision? A true vision?"

"Yes. Wouldn't you agree?"

"No! I'd think, maybe, the old guy was in cahoots with this Brother Paul, and had helped him end his life. It's not easy to hang yourself; it goes much better with an accomplice." He thought for a moment, then added, "Or maybe the old guy murdered Brother Paul for some reason. Like for some unpaid rhythmic gymnastics bet."

Rowan shook his head. "No. No. I worked with Brother Abelard to discover what had happened. We established that Brother Victor could not have done either of the things that you suggested—the assisted suicide, or the murder." He added with finality, "We concluded that Brother Victor had had a true vision."

The trooper shook his head. "But you described Brother Paul as troubled. Did you mean, like, despondent?"

Rowan conceded, "I suppose."

"Then Brother Victor may have picked up on subtle clues. Subconscious clues. Clues that led him to think that Brother Paul was contemplating suicide."

Rowan answered evenly. "You are welcome to your own interpretation of events, of course. But I'll stick with mine."

The car fell silent until Janice told Trooper Bateman, "I found a car rental place on Broad Street. Can you drop me off?"

He nodded. "Sure."

"Can we drop off Mister Butler first?" She turned to ask Rowan, "Is that okay with you? I'll come back and get you with the rental car tomorrow morning? Around nine-thirty?"

He answered, "Sure. I'd appreciate the alone time."

Janice handed him a metal key with a round red sticker on its side. The sticker bore the words: *office front door*. She said, "This will get you in."

The police cruiser pulled over on the Seventh Street side of the law offices, and Rowan got out. He said, "Thank you, Trooper."

Trooper Bateman replied, "You're welcome, sir." He started to drive off, but stopped when Janice put a hand on his arm.

She said, "Wait. I want to make sure he gets inside." She watched Rowan climb the steps, insert the key in the door lock, and enter without difficulty. Then she told the trooper, "He's in. Thank you," and they pulled away.

Rowan entered the reception area and stopped still, taking in the silence. He stared up at the ceiling mural for many minutes, admiring its beauty. As he did, he listened for the sound of any other occupants in the building; he concluded that he was indeed alone.

Rowan stuck his head into the meeting room and looked around, but he did not enter. He walked quietly back through the reception area, down the corridor, and into his small bedroom. He pulled off his tie, and his blazer, and his shoes, but he kept on his new and very comfortable underwear and socks. Then he began his pre-sleep ritual, clenching and unclenching his muscles in precise order until, for the first time in twenty years, he fell asleep in the broad daylight.

This time, a dream arrived with less intensity. He was back at the Community, but it lay beneath him in a soft focus. He floated over the massive bakery building and then swooped into the residence hall through an open window. His former self, Brother Thomas, was asleep in there on a narrow cot, on top of a coarse green blanket. The other twenty cots in the long room were empty. He hovered over his body until it opened its eyes suddenly, in alarm. This caused him to do the same thing in real life, back on his bed in Richmond. It took him half a minute to orient himself; to remember where he was. He kept still and listened to a noise from the other side of the wall, a tinny noise that was followed by a scraping sound.

Once he had determined the source of the noise, Rowan hopped from the bed, pulled on his pants, and walked out of the bedroom in his stocking feet. He pushed open the outside door and turned toward the alcove, feeling the hard pavement beneath him. He halted after a few steps and leaned back. He saw the same man he had seen the day before, the man in the *North Face* windbreaker, back inside the

Dumpster harvesting cans and bottles.

Rowan called to him, "Hello! Do you remember me?"

The man stopped his work and looked down. After a moment, he answered, "Did somebody steal your shoes?"

Rowan looked at his feet. "No! I left them inside. In my room."

The man jerked his thumb in the direction of the office building. "What? You live here?"

"I do. For now."

"They don't try to kick you out?"

"Who?"

"I don't know. The owners?"

"*I'm* the owner." Rowan took two more steps toward the man, who eyed him suspiciously.

The man said, "You're the owner of this here building?"

"So they tell me."

The man held out his arms and asked, "Well, okay. Do you mind if I scrounge for cans here?"

Rowan assured him, "No. Certainly not. I might even help you."

The man's wary look returned. Rowan pointed behind the Dumpster. "There was a guy asleep back there yesterday. A guy in overalls. Do you remember him?"

The man cast a worried glance at the spot. He shook his head rapidly.

Rowan prodded him. "No? Do you know him?"

The man declared, "I ain't got nothing to do with him. I mind my own business."

Rowan said, "Sure. Okay." He smiled. "Well, do you want some help with those cans?"

The man laughed. "Are you serious?"

"I am."

The man pointed to Rowan's pleated slacks. He said, "No. You ain't dressed for it."

Rowan offered, "I have another outfit, a simpler outfit, that I could change into."

"No. No, I got this covered." The man paused for a moment, then said, "Hey. I've been thinking about that fancy lady who was with you yesterday. The young one?"

He waited for Rowan to acknowledge whom he meant. "Yes. That was Janice."

"Well, your Miss Janice has some wrong ideas about me. There's reasons why people can't get a job." He added, "Nobody wants to work in a goddamn Dumpster."

"No. I'm sure not."

"I was in the Army. That's a job all right. That's a goddamn important job. More important than anything she's doing."

The man looked down into the Dumpster and then up at the sky. After a moment, he said, "Look, uh, it's getting late. I'll be fighting the rats for this stuff if I don't get done soon."

Rowan backed away. "Sure. I'll leave you to it. It was nice talking to you."

The man stared hard at Rowan, trying to determine if he was serious, or if he was mocking him. He finally said, "Yeah. Okay. You, too."

Rowan retraced his steps inside until he was seated on the bed. He removed the rest of his Brooks Brothers attire, including his socks and underwear, and stood naked for a moment. He draped the pants and shirt across the top of the chair and kicked the socks and underwear into a corner. Then he opened the blue-and-gold shopping bag, removed his robe and sandals, and put them on.

Rowan placed his ear against the wall and listened again for the tinny, scraping sounds outside. But they were gone. So he sat down again, pulled out MacDermott's legal file, and began to read.

Wednesday

It was closer to ten o'clock when Janice pulled up to the offices of MacDermott and Richman driving a white Ford Focus. Rowan was waiting for her outside, dressed once again in full Brooks Brothers attire.

Janice rolled down the window and told him, "I like that outfit, Rowan, but you need to have more than one. We need to go shopping again."

"This is my new uniform."

"How's that?"

"I've exchanged one uniform for another," Rowan explained. "A monk's habit for a Brooks Brothers suit. Same idea." He bent and peered into the interior of the Focus. "Is this your new car?"

"My rental. It's humbling, but it's free until I get my insurance check." Janice pointed to the passenger seat and told him, "Come on. We have a long way to go today, and lot to do."

Rowan walked around, climbed in, and buckled his seatbelt. Janice pointed into the back seat, at a paper bag marked *Kohlmann's Market*. "I picked up a few things for the trip. And for you."

Rowan took hold of the bag and pulled it up onto his lap. "That's very thoughtful. Thank you."

"It's some fresh fruit, a baguette, and bottles of water, so we don't have to stop."

"Okay. Then when will we get to Charleston?"

Janice checked her side mirror and pulled away. "Mister MacDermott called it a six-hour trip, but I'd call it five and a half." She nodded her head at the bag. "You'll see that I also got some shaving cream and a pack of razors. Disposables. I hope they're okay."

"Sure. Why wouldn't they be?"

"I don't know. Some guys get really fussy about their razors. They get upset if you, like, shave your legs with them."

"Oh?"

"Or your armpits. Or anything really."

Janice reached into her clutch purse, removed a bubble-packed cell phone, and handed it to Rowan, saying, "Here. This is your temporary cell phone until we get you on the grid."

Rowan studied the packaging. "The grid?"

"Yes. You have no phone. You have no e-mail address. You have no Facebook page. And apparently you have never owned a car, signed a lease, or paid a bill."

"Is that bad?"

"It's extremely unusual. And it can work against you."

Rowan tore at the packaging, with little success. He took it between his teeth and tried to rip it. Finally, Janice reached into her purse again and produced a nail clipper. She told him, "Here. Cut a corner open with this."

After two more minutes, she snatched back the clippers with an impatient, "Give me that." While stopped at the traffic light, she took the bubble-wrapped package, held it between her knees, and pried it open. She handed it back to Rowan with an edge of sarcasm. "Was that so hard?"

Rowan turned the phone over in his hand. "Sorry."

Janice restored the clippers to her bag and apologized. "No. No, I'm sorry. That wasn't called for." After a few seconds, she explained, "I'm upset today. I just read a story about Laurence in the *Richmond Times-Dispatch.* They spelled his name with a *w.* So did his parents on the online funeral notice. He would not have liked that."

"Would he have preferred Lance?"

"Probably. He'd have preferred Lance in the newspaper article anyway."

"What about in the funeral notice?"

"Maybe. I don't know if I'd have gone *that* far if I were his parents, but I'd have put the damn *u* in his name. His parents knew he preferred the *u*."

Janice reflected for a moment, then said, "He used to tell his parents that I was his girlfriend."

"Really?"

"Yeah. That went on for years."

"Why would he do that?"

"So he wouldn't have to come out to them."

"Come out?"

She explained, "Reveal that he was gay;" then added, "But I think they knew. They had to know. Everybody else did."

"And did you go along with . . . this ruse?"

"That I was his girlfriend?"

"Yes."

"I did. A little. When we were in our *friend* stage."

"Oh? How?"

"Maybe I'd dance with him at a bar mitzvah. Something like that."

Rowan thought this over, then asked, "So when is his funeral?"

"Tomorrow afternoon at three o'clock. Jews like to bury people quickly."

"Is it in Richmond?"

"No. It's down in Savannah. I'd bring you along, but I think it might be weird."

"How so?"

"It'll be very small. Very Jewish. Definitely not open to the public. Laurence's parents were kind of ashamed of him."

After a pause, Rowan answered evenly, "My parents were ashamed of me."

Janice stole a glance at her passenger. "Were they?"

Rowan didn't answer, and the pair fell silent for a long stretch of Interstate 95. Janice finally asked, "Is everything okay?"

"What do you mean?"

"You're not talking. Are you mad because I said that thing

about your parents?"

"No. I'm just not talking. Monks don't talk much." He paused to consider, "Are *you* upset about something?"

"Well, yes. I'm upset about Laurence."

"Of course."

"I didn't see him much but, come on, I've known him for my entire life. And now he's dead." She added, "I feel like I should do something for him, but I have no idea what."

Rowan suggested, "You could get him a prayer card."

Janice scoffed. "Please! What about a fruitcake? Or a statue to bury in the front yard?"

"Saint Joseph?"

"Yes. How ridiculous is that?"

"That statue thing is pretty ridiculous." He added, "Unless it works. In which case, it's not."

Janice assured him, "No. It's still ridiculous." She added, "Like those prayer cards I bought for your parents."

Rowan looked puzzled. "What? When?"

"The day I . . . extricated you from the Community. Brother Abelard made me buy two prayer cards. And a fruitcake."

"Oh? Well, thank you."

"Thank the Law Offices of MacDermott and Richman."

Rowan asked, "So, what happened to the cards?"

"I guess I left them there, on that big dough-pounding table, when I ran out after you."

Rowan said, "Oh. And the fruitcake?"

"I left it there, too."

"Those were high-quality fruitcakes."

Janice countered, "They were still fruitcakes."

"True."

"The ultimate dysfunctional holiday gift. Just ask Brother Carl."

Rowan said, "But the perpetual prayer cards aren't ridiculous, or dysfunctional."

"I'd beg to differ there."

"We could make one out to *Laurence* with a *u*. Or even to *Lance*."

"No, thank you. I'm sorry, but that's ridiculous, too. And dysfunctional. It may even be anti-Semitic."

"Do you think so? What's wrong with your name being remembered, out loud, in perpetuity?"

Janice scoffed again. "Perpetuity? Do you mean until Brother Abelard finally gets put out of business?"

"Out of business? Why?"

"Seriously? That's not exactly the Amazon warehouse he's running out there. There's not a lot of walk-in traffic, either. Except for me. I'm surprised he's stayed in business this long."

"Well, the abbot's business ventures do tend to fail. But I don't think the Community itself will fail. Not entirely. To the contrary, I think more and more people will be attracted to it, and to the life it offers."

Rowan pointed from Janice's Apple Watch to her iPhone to the GPS screen on the car console. "Many people will reach the point where they can't take all these . . . gizmos anymore; this technology overload. They will reach the point where they reject it all as Orwellian. As evil. God warned David not to number the heads of the Israelites. What He meant was *do not quantify* everyone. Do not give everyone a phone number, and an email address, and . . . What was that other thing?"

"A Facebook page." It was Rowan's turn to scoff. Janice challenged him. "So people will overdose on technology, and turn away from it, and do what?"

"They will walk out the door, and just keep walking."

"Walking where?"

"To someplace without all the gizmos, and all the quantifying, and all the data gathering."

"To the Community?"

"Well, to *a* community. It needn't be Saint Francis. There are other communities. There are different religious orders.”

“You mean different types of monks?”

“Oh yes.”

“Like what?”

“Like . . . eremitic monks. They are solitary hermits.”

“Sounds like *aromatic*. But I’ll bet they’re not very aromatic.”

“Or cenobitic monks. They interact with the public.”

“Like your group.”

“Yes. Or Carthusian monks, who dedicate their lives to contemplating God while confined to small cells.”

Janice’s lip curled. “Yikes. I wouldn’t last long there.”

“No. Neither would I.”

“But, why would anybody subject himself, or herself, to that?”

“Because some people are desperate to simplify. To have order in their lives before their heads explode. I felt that need.”

“But then, afterward, after the twenty years or so, you no longer felt it?”

“That’s right.”

Janice paused and then asked, “So was your community, the Saint Francis Community, a good place to be?”

“Sure. Except when it was a bad place.”

“What do you mean?”

“It was a good place for me, until it wasn’t,” Rowan answered. “Until I stopped believing.”

“Ah. Here we go. Believing in what?”

“In monasticism. In religion. In God.”

Janice shot a quick glance at him. “What happened to change your mind?”

Rowan shrugged. “Reading. I had read too much. I knew too much to spend any more time at the Community shoveling horse manure, mumbling prayers, avoiding all the little fights.”

“Fights? Really? You had fights out there?”

“Oh sure.”

"What about?"

Rowan answered, "The same things all people fight about: power, love, money."

"Don't you take vows to leave those things behind when you enter?"

"We take vows, yes. We say words, but so what? There is no leaving those things behind. Not really. The person you were when you arrived is still inside you."

"So if you were power-hungry in the real world, you'd be power-hungry in the Community?"

"Yes."

"And if you lusted after others in the real world, you'd lust after others there?"

"Oh yes."

"You said there were homosexuals there. Did they ever, you know, act on it?"

"Yes. Certainly."

"What about heterosexuals?"

Rowan pointed out, "Well, there was only one woman."

"Sister Agnes?"

"Yes.

"Did she act on it?"

"Yes."

"With who?"

"With whom."

Janice chided him, "Seriously? You're correcting my grammar?"

Rowan laughed. "No. I'm stalling."

Janice thought for a moment and then squealed, "Oh my God! Rowan! She acted on it with you?"

He conceded, "Yes. But I don't think *acted on it* is accurate, since nothing happened. I'd say she *suggested* it."

"She suggested it to you, but you turned her down?"

"Yes."

Janice muttered, "Well, I've been there." She went on, "So how did she suggest it?"

Rowan put his hand to his face and stroked his chin. He remembered aloud, "We were in the barn, raking muck—"

"Romantic."

"When two horses started to, you know, mate, or breed. She became excited by it."

"But you were not?"

"Not at all. I was repelled."

"Well, what did she do?"

"She picked up a handful of straw from the floor, and she flung it at me, so that the straw stuck to the front of my robe."

"Smooth move. Where on your robe?"

"The middle part. The waist. And below."

"Below the waist!"

"Yes. And then she started to brush it off. Very slowly."

"Wow. This is good stuff."

"No, it wasn't good. It was bad. I ran out of there as fast as I could."

Janice changed to a serious tone. "Yes. Of course, it was bad. Did she let the matter drop after that?"

"No. She was persistent. She sat with me at prayers. I tried to move, but she followed me. I finally had to tell her right out."

"How did you tell her?"

"What do you mean?"

"There are different ways to tell someone to leave you alone. You know: kindly; gruffly; with a nice dinner."

"Well, if I had to choose one of those, I'd say *kindly*. I told her that she distracted me too much during prayers."

"I've heard worse. So, she accepted that?"

"Yes. Eventually. Later, she started sitting next to Brother Carl. I guess he didn't mind the distraction."

Janice opened her mouth wide and snapped it shut. "Brother Carl?

Yikes. Do you think they were . . . doing it?"

"What?"

"The horses thing?"

"No. I don't think so."

Janice agreed, "I don't think so, either. But they did sit together? Once a day? In prayers?"

"They sat together three times a day—Matins, Mid-days, and Vespers."

"You prayed three times a day?"

"Yes."

"Isn't that a lot?"

Rowan pointed out, "Not at all. The Talmud suggests that Jews pray three times a day."

"It does?"

"Yes. And Muslims, of course, are told to pray five times a day."

"Okay. Okay. That's what they're told. But tell me. You actually pray, to some supernatural, God-like being?"

"Yes."

"What about now? Now that you're out of there. Today. You still do?"

"Sure. I pray."

"But you said you stopped believing."

"I stopped believing in a personal God. That's delusional. But I still believe."

"In what?"

"In human ideals."

"Okay. What are those?"

"Ideals? They're from Plato."

"Never heard of them."

"No? Not Platonic love?"

"Oh yes! I've heard of that one. It's kind of a kiss-off."

"Is it? I don't know what that means. I do know that, when I need to make a decision, I look to an ideal; to the best possible version of something like *honesty* or *kindness* or *friendship*. I think hard about it, to the exclusion of everything else. To me, that's a form of praying."

"So you pray for guidance?"

"Yes."

"And sometimes, magical, mystical things happen?"

"Yes."

"Like what?"

Rowan looked out at the passing landscape. "Like a little blue car appearing over the horizon. Like a young woman getting out of it and asking questions of the abbot. Like her seeing me, chasing after me, and taking me away."

Three hours later, they pulled off Route 95 and Janice read the road sign aloud: "Welcome to Charleston. The River City."

Rowan replied, "It was named after King Charles the Second. Of England."

Janice said, "I know. So was the Cavalier King Charles Spaniel."

"What's that?"

"It's a cute little dog. My friend Marcie has one."

Rowan took in the information and went on, "Charles was kicked off of, and then restored to, the English throne in a pair of coups d'état."

"I did not know that."

"He wanted to thank his supporters in the second coup, the counter coup, so he made them the eight *Lords Proprietors* of Charleston."

"That was nice of him."

"Charleston remains the most English city in America. Prince Charles himself has visited it."

"With Diana?"

"No. I don't think so."

Janice said, "I remember Diana's wedding dress. Her bridal

bouquet, too."

They turned onto East Bay Street and rolled past a building designated as the *Old Exchange and Provost Dungeon*. This caused Rowan to remark, "Even after England lost the Revolutionary War, after Lord Cornwallis surrendered at Yorktown, British soldiers kept fighting to hold onto this one city."

Janice shook her head. "How do you remember so many things?"

Rowan answered, "That's what the brain is for. To remember things. And it *does* if you don't overload it with nonsense; with things not worth remembering."

"So, you just read something, and you remember it?"

"Yes."

"Do you have a photographic memory?"

Rowan shrugged. "I suppose. But aren't all memories photographic? Don't we all pull up pictures from the brain, from the memory, and look at them?"

Janice replied, "Yes, we do. It's just a matter of degree, Rowan. You said that when you were in the Community, you read an entire book every night. How long did that take you?"

"About two hours."

"And how much of each book would you remember?"

"How much? Why, all of it."

"There. You see? That's not normal."

"No?"

"No. It took me three weeks to read *Gone Girl*, and I only remember the sex stuff."

Rowan said, "I read that President Kennedy could skim-read one thousand words per minute."

Janice replied, "I read that he had satyriasis."

"What is that?"

"Uncontrollable sexual desire."

"Oh."

Janice drove into the Battery area. Rowan spotted a couple with a cart and pointed to them. He said, "Those are homeless people, right?"

"Right."

"And what about that guy next to them, sleeping on the grass?"

"Yeah. Him, too."

He paused and said, "You know, I don't recall seeing *any* homeless people when I was young."

Janice assured him, "The world has changed, a lot, in twenty years." Two blocks later, she pulled over and announced, "This is it. On our left. Your parents' Charleston mansion." Rowan craned his neck and stared up as high as he could. The house was massive, rising three stories to a large, octagonal cupola. The first two stories had white columns and low white railings, providing each level with a fifty-foot-wide porch. The creamy paint on the house continued around back to a ten-foot-high garden wall, giving the impression of one uninterrupted compound.

Rowan sat back. Janice told him, "According to my dad, Doran and Siobhan Butler spent very little time in this Charleston house. Or, for that matter, in any house."

"Oh? So where did they spend their time?"

"In hotels. In Ritz Carlton hotels."

Rowan turned to her. "But why would they do that?"

Janice shrugged. "Well, in a hotel, people make your bed for you; people pick up your towels; they make you food."

"But Doran and Siobhan could have hired people to do that here, and at the other place. Right?"

"Right."

Rowan turned over his palms. "And why Ritz Carlton hotels?"

"Well, as you know, they were world travelers. And there are Ritz Carltons all over the world. Doran was a major shareholder in Marriott International, which is the parent company of the Ritz." She added, "By the way, that means *you* are now a major shareholder in Marriott International."

Rowan muttered, "That seems like such a waste of money."

Janice paused and then said, "For you and me, yes. But they weren't like you and me; they were the super-rich. And maybe they figured: *You can't take it with you.* Maybe they decided to spend as much money as they possibly could."

Janice drove on past the front door of the property, turned right, and parked in the street alongside it. She asked Rowan, "Have you had a chance to study the house plans?"

"Yes, They were in my stack of legal papers."

She fished in her purse and pulled out a jangling keychain. "Then shall we go in?"

Rowan pointed to the ten-foot high garden wall. "Let's see what's in there first."

Janice fingered the keychain and held up a long, iron one. "Okay. This is the key to the garden door."

Before she got out, Janice gestured broadly to the garden and house, and told Rowan, "I don't know if this was in your papers, too, but you should know something: Your parents took part in the *Festival of Houses and Gardens* every year, for many years. Someone may contact you soon about continuing that tradition."

"What's the tradition?"

"Rich people in Charleston let poor people into their mansions."

Rowan said, "I like the sound of that,"

Rowan got out and walked up to the rough-hewn wooden door. He placed his hand on it and commented, "This is old. This feels very, very old."

"Yes. Dad told me that Siobhan found this door in a monastery in Ireland and loved-loved-loved it. So Doran bought it for her and shipped it back here. He was always doing stuff like that."

Janice stuck the key into the door lock, turned it, and pushed against the heavy door. It opened onto the first step of a stone path. She stood back to let Rowan enter first. Then she followed, leaving the door ajar.

Inside the garden, the cream-colored wall was not faring as well. Ugly splotches of lichen had spread across many areas, giving the wall an unhealthy, pockmarked look. A profusion of plants, native and exotic, flourished inside the walls to the point of nearly overwhelming it.

The thick vegetation was broken up by several small sitting areas with wrought iron benches big enough for two. Rowan's eye, however, was drawn immediately to the statuary. He counted four statues interspersed throughout the garden, each standing about five feet tall.

Janice noticed his interest. She pointed to the closest statue and said, "Look! It's like a garden gnome, but a tall one."

Rowan corrected her. "It's not a gnome; it's a saint." He pointed around to the three others. "They're all saints."

"Oh? Sorry."

"Curiously, they are all *monastic* saints."

Janice poked his arm. "And I'll bet you know who they are, of course."

"Of course. Every saint is depicted with an object that symbolizes his . . . specialty."

"Specialty? Like a doctor? Like rhinoplasty?"

"No. Like . . . if he was known for his great learning, or for his charitable works. That kind of thing." Rowan stopped at the nearest statue. "This is Saint Francis of Assisi."

"As in *the Saint Francis Community*?"

"Yes. Francis is always depicted with a bird in his hand." He moved on to a second one and said, "As opposed to Saint Anthony of Padua here, who is always depicted holding an infant."

Janice mumbled, "An un-diapered infant, I might add."

Rowan continued to wander. "Here is Saint Benedict, of the Benedictine Order. He always has this big shepherd's staff."

She mumbled even lower, "Showing off."

"Benedict is credited with the Latin motto *Ora et labora*, or *Pray and work.*"

"Catchy. You should share the Latin part with Kitty."

"And that one over there is Saint Dominic, the founder of the Dominican Order. He is traditionally depicted holding a Bible."

Janice walked behind the fourth statue. She asked Rowan, "How come they're all bald? And all bald in the same spot?"

"Tonsure."

"What?"

"Tonsure. It's a symbolic shaving of the head; a rejection of personal vanity."

Janice said, "It looks like male-pattern baldness. My dad had that, but he got plugs."

"Plugs?"

"Hair follicles from his neck, transferred to the top of his head. A lot of guys have that."

Rowan answered distractedly, "Oh," and continued to study the fourth statue.

Janice cast her gaze around the garden. Then she stopped, reached out, and touched Rowan's arm again. She asked him, in a hushed voice, "Hey, uh, is one saint traditionally shown sleeping on a bench?"

"No. Not that I've read about." Rowan followed Janice's gaze to a bench ten feet away. There was a man sitting on the wrought iron. His head was flopped back, and his mouth was hanging open, emitting a low, snoring sound.

In the next moment, Janice and Rowan acted on opposite impulses—she backing out of the garden, pulling out her phone, and dialing nine-one-one; he approaching the bench, sitting down, and studying the man who was sleeping on it.

Rowan estimated the man to be about his own age, though his stubbled face showed deep creases. He was dressed in a pair of blue overalls that were splotched, like the garden wall, with dark spots.

The man woke up slowly, closing his mouth and righting his head.

He turned toward Rowan and opened his eyes, revealing a spider web of red veins. He croaked, "Who are you?"

"I'm Rowan. They tell me I own this garden now."

The man swiveled his head and looked around. "Yeah? I thought this place belonged to Doran."

On hearing the name, Rowan's face registered surprise, and he leaned closer, regarding the man with heightened interest. "Yes. It did. Did you know Doran?"

"Yeah. I knew him pretty good."

Rowan said simply, "He was my father."

The man's red eyes widened. "No shit?"

Rowan answered, "No. None of . . . that." He added, "He just passed away, in a car accident."

"Yeah. I heard that. Him and his wife."

"Yes. My mother."

"Sorry, guy."

Rowan shifted on the bench and asked, "Maybe you can tell me: What was Doran like?"

The man placed his own head in his hands and squeezed hard. When he answered, it was in a sharper, more focused voice. "You'd know that better than me. Wouldn't you?"

Rowan nodded. "Normally, yes." He added, "But this isn't normally."

The man closed his eyes and lolled his head back and forth. He finally replied, "Yeah, I hear that, guy. Things weren't cool with you and your old man? I been there. But I can tell you this: Doran was very cool with the vets. Even with the fucked-up vets like me. He gave us work; he gave us beer when he was at the house." The man thought for a moment. "Though he wasn't at the house much." The man held out a pair of grimy hands. "He even let us crash out here on the benches."

"Is that right? He gave you permission to stay here?"

"He did."

Rowan studied the man's face. Then he told him, "I have seen you before."

The man studied him back. "Well, I didn't see you, guy."

"No. You didn't. You were asleep behind a Dumpster. Up in Richmond."

The man protested, "Richmond? No, not me. You saw somebody else."

Before Rowan could reply, Janice returned to the garden. She kept her distance from the bench and announced, "Okay. The police are on their way."

It was Rowan who looked alarmed. "The police? Why?"

Janice explained, as if it were obvious, "This man is trespassing. He had to scale a ten-foot wall to get in here. This is clearly private property, and he is trespassing on it."

"Oh? I don't think that's so clear."

"Rowan! It's just like he broke into your house." She pointed to the old wooden door. "That door is kept locked for a reason."

"What is the reason?"

"How about to keep thieves from breaking in, and stealing your things, and harming you?"

Janice turned and faced the entrance. Within seconds, she heard the sound of a car pulling up, followed by the sound of a door opening and closing. A large black woman, in a dark green uniform, ducked under the garden's archway and approached the group. She asked, "Did somebody here call nine-one-one?"

Janice responded, "Yes. I did."

"About an intruder?"

In response, Janice pointed to the bench. The policewoman stood to her full height of six feet and strode forward. She looked down at the two men seated on the bench and surmised, "I suppose it's the scruffy one." She turned to Janice, "What do you want me to do?"

"What do you mean?"

"You want me to run him off? Or arrest him?"

Rowan replied, "We don't want either one."

Janice snapped at him, "Rowan! He could be crazy. He probably is!"

Rowan turned to the man and asked, "Are you crazy?"

"No, guy."

Janice appealed to the police officer. "Can you help us out here?"

The policewoman asked her, "Well, what do you want to happen?"

"Can he be taken away for some reason?"

"Like for being crazy?"

"Yes."

The policewoman looked hard at the man on the bench. She asked him, "What's your name?"

He answered, with some reluctance, "My name's Steve. Steve Kowalski."

"Where do you live, Steve Kowalski?"

"No fixed abode."

"You're homeless?"

"That's right."

The policewoman took out a small pad and pen and scribbled a note. Then she looked back at him. "All right. Name the current president of the United States."

Rowan moaned, "Oh no. Here we go again."

Steve Kowalski laughed a broken-toothed laugh and answered, "President? I don't know. Is it still Trump? I don't really follow politics."

Rowan said, "Listen, officer. This garden is my property. This man is on my property."

The policewoman turned to Janice, who affirmed that fact. Rowan continued, "I just learned that my father, the previous owner, invited this man to come here. I now extend the same invitation. Does that resolve the problem?"

The policewoman replied, "This is your place? And you don't

mind him being here?"

"No. He is as welcome here as Jesus."

Her eyes opened upon hearing the divine name. She turned to Janice and explained, "Since *you* called *me*, I still have to run a background check on this man." The policewoman pointed at Steve Kowalski and told him, "You. Come with me now."

He growled, "Come with you where?"

The officer eyeballed him. She answered sharply, "To the back seat of my patrol car, unless you got warrants out for you, in which case we're going to the police station. *Do you* have any outstanding warrants?"

"No."

"Then you should be back on your bench soon."

Rowan and Janice watched them go. Rowan said, "This is good. This is *de lege ferenda*."

"What?"

He translated it. "*The law as it should be*. As opposed to *de lege late.*"

Janice answered impatiently, "Oh yes, of course. *Da mocha latte*."

He translated it. "*The law as it is*."

She pulled back, annoyed. "Seriously, Rowan? You think this is good?"

"Yes."

"You seriously want a stumblebum sleeping here in your garden?"

"A stumblebum?"

"Yes. A homeless, unemployed, drug addict, if you prefer."

"I think it's the right thing to do. My father welcomed him here."

Janice threw up her hands. "Then, as they say, Rowan: It's your funeral. I've got one funeral to attend; why not make it two?"

"All I'm doing is extending hospitality to the poor."

Janice pointed to the house. "Hospitality? What is this, a Holiday Inn?"

"No. But it could be a respite for . . . for the weary. Like the

Hospitalers had."

"The who?"

Rowan explained, "Technically, the Order of Knights of the Hospital of Saint John of Jerusalem."

Janice rolled her eyes. "Oh right. Them."

"They founded a hospital in Jerusalem a thousand years ago. They dedicated it to Saint John the Baptist."

Janice said, "I went to Jerusalem with Mom, Dad, and Bubbe. It was a disaster. We refer to it now as *The Six-Day War*."

"They served the weary travellers to the Holy Land. They treated every pilgrim who walked through the door like he was Jesus Himself."

"Mom and Dad weren't getting along at all. Sparks were flying. And Bubbe was throwing gasoline on the sparks."

The policewoman strode back into the garden with Steve Kowalski in tow. She said, "No outstanding warrants, so he's all yours. Ya'll have a good day now."

Janice said, "Thank you, ma'am," and then amended it to, "Thank you, Officer." The policewoman turned and exited quickly. Janice, Rowan, and Steve Kowalski listened to her pull out and drive away. Once she was gone, Janice told Rowan, "I have to call Mister MacDermott and give him an update. I'll leave you two to . . . bond? I don't know." She exited the garden, too, and walked out to her car.

Rowan escorted Steve Kowalski back to the bench. Steve grumbled, "Shit. I thought we were in the South, man."

"What do you mean?"

"Seriously? A nigger cop jacking me up like that? And a female one at that? Where's she get off disrespecting a white veteran? And a male one at that?" Taken aback, Rowan just stared at him, as he continued. "I thought they had it together down here. Not like up home."

Rowan replied cautiously. "Oh? And where is home?"

"Pennsylvania. Up in the northeast part."

"Oh? Is that coal country?"

"Used to be, guy. Now it's meth country. The whole meth thing started up there, at least for east-coast tweakers."

"Tweakers?"

"Meth addicts!"

"Oh."

"I got caught up in it when I was just outta high school. I did a few months in county lockup for selling rocks. No big deal, though. The Army took me anyway."

Rowan gestured that his guest should sit on the bench, which he did, followed by Rowan. After a moment, Rowan asked him, "So what did you do in the Army?"

Steve Kowalski stared at the ground. "Same as I was doing before I went in. I was a mechanic—cars, trucks, buses—I worked on them all. I was in a motor pool over in the desert; mostly cleaning sand and shit out of engines. I was doing good, too. I got promoted two times. Then things turned bad. A couple of the new guys started tweaking."

Rowan interjected, "Smoking meth."

"Yeah. So old stupid Steve here started smoking with them. I got busted in one week."

"Really? A week?"

"Yeah. You can't be fucked-up over there. It's too fucking dangerous."

"Did they arrest you?"

"Sort of." Steve looked at him. "But I played it smart. Before they could charge me officially, I self-identified. That means *I* told *them* I was a drug addict before *they* could tell *me*."

"I see. So you got an honorable discharge?"

Steve laughed hoarsely. "Nothing's that simple in the military, guy. Why use two words when you can use ten, right? I got discharged *under conditions other than dishonorable.*"

"And how long ago was that?'

"Depends on what year this is, I guess."

Rowan nodded. He said, "Okay. So, what do you do now?"

"I got a wife and kid, guy. So that's what I do." He spit on the ground, then added, "My wife's got anger issues. Big time. And my kid's a fucking mess, naturally." Steve looked into Rowan's eyes and told him, "I got a good prospect in Charleston, though. There's a bus company that hires vets. I'm going there tomorrow to talk to the boss. He's an old motor pool man."

The two sat in silence for a minute until Rowan asked, "So what will you do today?"

Steve answered calmly, "Today? I don't know. I might go to the library and read."

"Ah! Really? I'm a great reader myself."

"Well, I'm not so great. But if I start a book, and I get into it, I might spend a week plowin' through it."

Rowan asked him, "A book like what?"

"Like *For Whom the Bell Tolls*. That had a great ending, man. Now *that's* the way to die."

"Yes! I remember that ending."

"And like *Strangers on a Train*."

Rowan shook his head. "Haven't read it."

"And like *Crime and Punishment*. Have you read that one?"

"By Dostoevsky?"

"Is that how you say it?"

"Yes. I *have* read it. You did, too?"

"It took a while, but yeah, I read it. Dude got away with a murder, for awhile, but then he got punished in the end." He added, "I guess we all do."

At that moment, Janice re-entered the garden and walked up to the bench. She told Rowan, "Mister MacDermott wants us to go inside and to check the items in there against the inventory list." She shot a quick glance at Steve Kowalski. "To make sure nothing has been stolen."

Steve Kowalski, apparently not offended, stood and said to Rowan, "Sounds like you got some business to take care of. I'll be pushing off."

Rowan stood with him. "To the library?"

"Maybe. Maybe to the park."

"Well, where are you sleeping tonight?"

He pointed back at the bench. "Right there, if you'll let me."

Rowan told him, "No."

Steve Kowalski pulled back. "No? Well, okay."

Rowan grinned, "No, I mean you must come inside."

Janice sputtered, "Rowan!"

"In fact, come inside with us now and pick a room. We have plenty of them. You'll stay here tonight."

Janice breathed in and out slowly to calm herself. Then she fished a set of keys out of her purse and led the two men out of the garden and up to a side door. She told Rowan, "We can go in this way. This is the servants' entrance."

Rowan did not reply, but Steve Kowalski did. "That works for me. I ain't proud."

Janice frowned, inserted a key, and opened the door onto a very large, country-style kitchen. She paused to admire the stainless steel appliances as Rowan and Steve Kowalski walked past her, through the dining room, and into the foyer.

By the time Janice re-joined them, Rowan was pointing up a wide mahogany staircase and saying, "You can stay up there, in that first room on the left."

Janice objected. "Wait! That's the master bedroom!"

Rowan turned to her. He said, "Yes. Why? Did you want that one? The one next to it is just as big. You can have that."

"No I don't want that one! I want to be someplace safe. I want to be as far away from two strange men as I can possibly get."

Rowan seemed genuinely puzzled. He asked her, "Why?"

"Why? Because a young woman has to worry about . . . such

things."

Rowan assured her, "Well, you needn't worry about me."

Steve Kowalski spoke up. "Me, either. I can't get it up no more. Ask my wife. I smoked too much meth." With a final grin, he walked up the stairs, turned left, and disappeared into the master bedroom.

Janice muttered, "E. D. I'm not surprised."

Rowan asked, "What's that?"

"Erectile Dysfunction. It's more common than you know." Janice shook her head ruefully. "All right. I'll take the maid's room off of the kitchen. It has a deadbolt lock."

"Okay."

Janice told him, "You should stay upstairs and keep an eye on your *houseguest*," putting air quotes around her final word. Then she looked around the foyer, crinkled her nose, and added, "Oh no."

"What"

"There's mold in here. I can smell it."

Rowan tilted his head back and sniffed. "I can't."

"I'm very sensitive to it."

The foyer was large and square in shape, and painted in a soft yellow hue. The right wall featured a large painting of a soldier on a horse; the left wall had an equally large painting of a woman sitting in a flower garden. In the center of the right wall was a door, currently open, leading into a study. The left wall had a similar door, currently closed, that led into a parlor.

Janice strolled over toward the study. She rapped on the wall with her knuckles and told Rowan, "We'll need to hire someone to cut into these boards and check for mold spores." She turned and pointed to the front. "We'll need someone to upgrade these windows, too."

Rowan approached a set of tall window between the front door and the parlor. He placed his fingers on the cold glass. "Why? What's wrong with the windows?"

"Well, look at them. They're just regular glass with metal locks, probably fifty years old. I'll bet all the windows in the house are like that. Someone could easily break the glass and climb in."

"Why would they do that?"

"Did you see the inventory list?"

"I did."

"This house is full of expensive things—artwork, furniture, clocks, tchotchkes."

"What are those?"

"Knick-knacks."

Rowan peered into the study. "Okay. So who do we hire to fix those things? Should I ask Steve?"

"No! Are you kidding?"

"No."

Janice shook her head disapprovingly. Then she told him, "I will take care of it. I belong to Hannah's List. I'll get on and find us the best local contractor."

"Whose list?"

"Hannah's."

"That's another palindrome: *Hannah*."

Janice pulled out her phone and aimed it at Rowan. "Hannah's List identifies the best contractors in an area. It calls out the worst ones, too."

"This Hannah woman decides who is the best and the worst?"

"No. The customers do. They write in and vote for the best. Or they trash the worst." She smiled. "Those bad reviews can be pretty funny."

"Isn't it possible that contractors vote for themselves?"

"What? How?"

"They pretend to be customers, and they say nice things about themselves."

"I guess that could happen. But I would hope not."

Rowan told her, "We had something like that at the Community. Brother Abelard told us to vote for an employee of the month, explaining that it should be the person who had worked the hardest that month. But when he counted up the votes, he discovered that some monks had written in their own names, multiple times; some even disguised their handwriting to do so. We only had twenty-five members of the Community back then, but Brother Abelard received over sixty votes. So we did not have an employee of the month that month. Or any other month."

Janice, who was clicking through screens on her phone, muttered, "Jeez, you'd think monks would be honest. Where's the hope for the rest of us?" Then she looked up and said, "Okay, I've found the best contractor: Finn Mahoney. He specializes in restoration of older homes, with mold, and he has all top ratings."

Rowan said, "Good. Call him," as he wandered over to the parlor.

Janice keyed in a number and spoke to the contractor for five minutes. When she joined Rowan, he turned to her and observed, "You look puzzled."

Janice held up her phone and replied, "I think Finn Mahoney is a woman."

"Well, is that all right?"

Janice concluded, "Sure. Why not? We're meeting him, or her—" She paused. "You know, let's just say *her* now because I'm sure she was a woman. At least I'm ninety percent sure. I've been fooled before. Anyway, we're meeting her for lunch."

Steve Kowalski suddenly appeared in the doorway, which caused Janice to flinch. He asked Rowan, "Hey, guy. You got any beer?"

Janice answered, "No. We don't."

Steve Kowalski continued to address Rowan. "Bummer. You need beer. Everybody does."

Rowan smiled tightly and said, "Sorry."

Steve Kowalski waited a moment, then asked, "You want me to go get some?"

Janice opened her mouth, but Rowan beat her to the answer. "All right."

"I'll need some money."

Rowan answered, "Yes, of course," and turned to Janice. "Do you have any cash?"

Janice sputtered, "No! Or very little. I don't carry cash."

"None at all?"

"Well . . . just . . . my mad money."

"What's that?"

"You know: If you're on a date, and you get mad at your date, and you have to pay for a ride home."

"Oh. Can I have some of that money for Steve? I'll pay you back. With interest."

Janice blew a blast of air from her mouth to her nose. Then, very reluctantly, she reached into her pocket and pulled out a five-dollar bill. Steve Kowalski commented, "That won't buy much beer. Not at that place around the corner."

Janice retracted the bill and pulled out a ten. "This will have to do."

He took the bill. "Yes, ma'am. Can I get you anything?"

"No."

Steve Kowalski exited the room; they heard him leave the house via the front door.

Janice raised her eyes and her hands to heaven. Then she lowered both, shook her head, and leveled a stare at Rowan. She told him, "While he's gone, let's talk about the inventory list. Mister MacDermott is on my case about that." She gestured around the parlor. "Doran and Siobhan, or at least Siobhan, had an eye for fine things. She had many things shipped from Europe and Asia to the houses in Charleston and Savannah."

Rowan stroked the material of a chair. "Is that where this furniture came from?"

"Possibly."

"Is it very valuable?"

"I would think so, but we should really hire someone to catalogue it all and to tell us what it's worth. I know nothing about furniture, and I expect you know less than I do."

Rowan replied, "Well, I only know what I've read." He tapped the chair in front of him. "These are called Queen Anne chairs. You can tell by the wings at the top. Those leather ones by the fireplace are Chesterfields. And the chairs around the dining room table back there? Those are Chippendales."

Janice sighed. She muttered, "I got sat on once by a Chippendale."

"What?"

"The male stripper type. It was at a bachelorette party. For Wendy Brill."

"Chippendale is a breed of horse, too."

"He got on top of Wendy like he was riding a horse. And he started beating her with a leather crop. We all laughed, but it was kind of disturbing."

Steve Kowalski appeared in the doorway again; startling Janice again. He was holding a six-pack of Corona beer under his arm and a stick of Beef Jerky in his hand. He looked at Janice, and then at Rowan. "Good night, you two. I'll be heading up."

Rowan waved and said, "Good night."

Janice did not speak. She rolled her eyes, walked briskly out the front door, and returned one minute later with her paper bag from Kohlmann's. She sat in one of the wing chairs and pointed Rowan to the other. Once they were both seated, she pulled out two bottles of water, two apples, and a baguette, inquiring, "Is this okay for dinner tonight?" She glanced upstairs and added, "I'd rather not go out. Not with him here."

Rowan took a water bottle and an apple from her. He conceded, "Sure."

"We should just sit and talk about some things; some important things. Okay?"

"Important things like Steve Kowalski?"

"No. Hey, what you *do* and *don't do* here are your decisions. I can only advise you."

"Okay. So what's on your mind?"

Janice answered, "Laurence Myers' murder."

Rowan nodded rapidly. "Yes, of course."

Janice said, "Here's what bothers me about that: The police said it was a random killing, in a high-crime drug area."

"But you say it was not."

"I *know* it was not."

"Why?"

"Because Laurence did not do drugs. Never. Ever. He looked down on people who did."

"Then what do you think happened?"

Janice broke the baguette in half and handed him a piece. She said, "Rowan, I think that . . . whoever killed Laurence was really trying to kill you."

After a stunned pause, he replied, "Me?"

"Think about it: Laurence had your red hair, and your basic build. He was sitting in a car that *you* had been sitting in just hours before. If someone had seen you after the salon, after Brooks Brothers, that someone would know all he'd need to know to follow you, and then to kill you."

"But . . . Who would want to kill me?"

Janice brandished the piece of bread. "Take your pick! Either of your half-siblings would. Kitty is a psycho. Ewell will do whatever she tells him to do."

"Okay." Rowan considered her words. Then he warmed to the topic. "Okay. I can understand *their* motive. But . . . Who else is there? Who else had a motive to kill me? What about Mark Richman?"

Janice seemed surprised. "My father?"

"Yes. Kitty said she would ruin your father if she didn't get her money."

"But Dad? No! Not Dad. He would never kill anybody."

"No?"

"No."

Rowan held out a hand to placate her. "Okay. Then what about Mister MacDermott?"

Janice took a bite of apple and chewed it, so Rowan did the same. She finally spoke, "Maybe. I don't really know who Mister MacDermott is. I never have."

"How's that?"

"He seems to be one thing, but he's really another."

"There are a lot of people like that."

"Tell me about it." Janice paused for a moment; then went on. "One night, after he had had too many drinks, Dad told me that Mister MacDermott had been in love with Siobhan Kelly."

"My mother?"

"Yes." She looked him in the eyes. "Are you sure you want to hear about this?"

"Yes. Absolutely."

"Well, my dad said that Siobhan was more than MacDermott's secretary; she was his protégé, and possibly even his lover, until Doran stole her away."

Rowan alternated bites of bread and apple for several minutes. Then he said, "I need to think about this. This is . . . many-faceted."

Janice agreed. "It is."

Rowan gathered up his dinner items and stood. He said, "I'll go find a bedroom upstairs." He added, "Unless you want me to sleep downstairs. You know? Because of the windows?"

Janice told him, "No. You should go upstairs. But lock your door. And stay away from the window; from *all* windows."

"Why?"

"Because someone might try to shoot you."

"Really?"

"Yes. Really."

Rowan walked past her into the foyer. He muttered, "All right. I will. Good night then."

Janice hoisted up her water bottle as if in salute. "Good night."

At nine AM, Janice entered the kitchen and said, "Good morning, Rowan." But the man standing at the sink in the Brooks Brothers suit turned around and proved to be someone else. Janice pulled back and nearly shouted, "Mister Kowalski?"

He told her, "You can just call me Steve."

Janice made several hand gestures before thinking of something to say. "Well, you certainly look different."

"Yeah. I got a job interview today."

"Oh? Good for you."

"Rowan thought my overalls looked too bad to wear. These threads look too good, but what are you gonna do?"

"Right. Better to go with *too good*."

Steve Kowalski looked past Janice and called out, "Hey! Look at you, guy!"

Janice spun around. She bulged her eyes out and held them there, like a cartoon frog, at the sight. For Rowan was once again wearing his monk's robe and sandals.

Steve said, "Hey! You look like one of them gnomes out in the garden."

Rowan corrected him. "Those are saints."

Janice recovered enough to mutter, "I just hope you're wearing underwear this time."

He assured her, "I am. Very expensive underwear." He pointed to the man wearing his suit. "Steve is applying for a job with a bus company. He doesn't look crazy anymore, does he?"

Janice swallowed and replied, "No. He doesn't." She added, "And why would he? He's wearing a thousand-dollar suit."

Rowan told Steve Kowalski. "Good luck today."

"Thanks, man. I appreciate the threads. They're killer."

Rowan extended his hands and flipped them over. He asked, "Do you need any cash today? For a taxi maybe?"

Steve Kowalski looked furtively at Janice, then answered, "Sure. Okay."

Janice tensed, but then she reached into her pocket, this time producing a twenty-dollar bill. She handed it to him without comment, but she did tell Rowan, "You and I need to get to a bank."

Steve Kowalski started out. Rowan called after him, "Come back as soon as you're done. We want to hear how it went."

He replied, "Will do. Shouldn't take too long." He held up the twenty-dollar bill, waved it at them, and exited through the servants' door.

After a few seconds, Janice gestured to Rowan that he should follow her. They, too, exited by the servants' door and climbed into her rental car. Janice drove six blocks in silence, then pulled over and parked. She gestured again for Rowan to follow, which he did, and they were soon standing before a Wells Fargo Bank. Janice pointed at a machine in front of them and said, "Do you know what that is?"

Rowan admitted, "No."

"It's an ATM machine."

Rowan pondered for a moment. "I'm guessing the *M* already stands for *Machine*."

"Yes. So?"

"So it's redundant to say ATM *machine*."

"Whatever. You owe me thirty dollars."

"What do the *A* and *T* stand for?"

Janice replied testily. "I don't know!" She then amended her response to, "I think they stand for *Automated* and *Teller*. It's a machine that automatically gives you money, like a teller."

Rowan smiled. "Like a robot teller."

"Yes. Listen: You now have a checking account right here at Wells Fargo."

"I do?"

"Yes. Mister MacDermott set it up last night. All you have to do is think of a PIN number."

"What's that?"

"It's a secret code. Something that gives you, and only you, access to your account."

"But what does PIN mean?"

Janice bit her tongue, then answered, "It means Personal Identification Number."

"So the letter *N* already stands for *Number*?"

"Yes! You can contemplate that great truth later, Rowan. Okay? For now, you need to think of a four-digit number. Make sure it is something you could not possibly forget."

After a moment's contemplation, Rowan said, "Okay. I got it."

Janice pointed to the keypad and directed him, "Type it in." He did, and followed a set of prompts. Janice then showed him how to extract five twenty-dollar bills. He immediately handed two of them over to her.

Janice took the bills and said, "Thank you. Now I owe you a ten."

Rowan shook his head. "No. No need. That's interest."

"Ten dollars interest? On thirty dollars? Wouldn't that be usury?"

Rowan looked at her in surprise. "Usury? Where did you hear that word?"

Janice replied, "From that little nun. The manic one at the Community."

"Sister Agnes?"

"Yes."

Rowan turned back to the ATM. He asked, "Can I take out as much money as I want?"

Janice clenched her teeth. She replied, "No! Thank God. There is a cash limit."

"What's the limit?"

"Mister MacDermott set it up for one hundred dollars a day." She paused, then asked him, "Can you live on that?"

Rowan replied, "I can live on zero dollars a day. I have for many years."

At twelve noon, Janice drove herself and Rowan up Meeting Street to an indoor-outdoor café called The Barrister. Janice peered through the café's windows to check that Finn was not already inside. She and Rowan then took up positions next to the curb and waited. After a moment, Janice asked, "So, just curious, what is your PIN number?"

"Am I allowed to tell you? Isn't it a secret?"

"It is a secret. You shouldn't tell anybody. I'm just afraid you'll forget it, so you might want me as a backup."

"I don't forget things."

"Yeah. I'm starting to realize that."

After a moment, Rowan told her, "It's *ten eighteen*. One-zero-one-eight."

"Okay. Why that number?"

"Because Janice starts with *J*, and that's the tenth letter in the alphabet. Richman starts with *R*, the eighteenth letter." He added, "You said to pick something I would never forget."

Janice answered quietly, "Oh."

A large Ram 250 pickup truck, black with a chrome running board, rumbled past them and angle-parked across the road. A young woman with close-cropped hair hopped down from the cab, locked the door, and crossed the street at a jaunty gait.

Janice said, "That's Finn."

"How do you know?"

"Because she looks like someone who might sound like a man on the phone." She waved and called, "Here we are, Finn!"

The woman waved back. She was tall and muscular, and she wore no make-up on her lightly freckled face. She took in Rowan's figure and called out, "Dude, are you a monk?"

"I used to be."

"Seriously? Wow. You look like one of those medieval fair guys. You know? The ones that sell the turkey legs? Hey, do you have shoes on?" Rowan raised his robe enough to reveal his sandals.

Finn continued, "Cool. And how about underwear?"

Rowan smiled. "Yes, but you'll have to take my word for that."

"I will. Wow."

Janice extended her hand and they shook. "I'm Janice Richman, of the MacDermott and Richman law firm. We'll be paying for your work on the house and the garden."

"Cool. I'm Finn. It's really Finola, but no one calls me that." She winked at Rowan. "No one calls me that and lives anyway."

A young man in a white shirt and black vest emerged from the restaurant and addressed them. "Would you folks like to sit outside or in?"

Rowan examined the two rows of light metal tables to his right and turned to the others, "What do you think?"

Finn assured him, "It don't make no nevermind to me."

Just at that moment, a couple clattered past them pushing a shopping cart full of cans. This prompted Janice to tell the waiter, "I'd rather not look at that."

The waiter looked back at her blankly and did not reply. Rowan made the decision. "We'll take a table outside." He told Janice, "You can sit with your back to the street and see no evil." He led the trio to the closest table and sat. Janice stared at the table grumpily and then settled in across from Rowan. Finn, looking puzzled, took the seat between the two.

They remained in awkward silence for ten seconds until the waiter announced, "The luncheon special today is fresh-caught, Atlantic-waters fish and chips." With no deliberation, Janice, Finn, and Rowan all ordered that special along with a glass of white wine for Janice, a glass of beer for Finn, and a glass of water for Rowan.

After the waiter departed, Janice looked out at the street and commented, "Speaking of homeless, I expect to see your new friend driving by any minute now, in a taxi."

When Rowan did not reply, Finn asked, "What do you mean?"

Janice explained, "Rowan has been handing money to a bum."

Before Rowan could react, she corrected herself, "Excuse me, to a homeless man, who is down on his luck, who must drink six beers in order to go to sleep at night."

Rowan told Finn, "He's a veteran who needed money."

Janice continued, "Okay. But you can't just walk around handing it to people. People need to work for their money."

Rowan smiled. "But I didn't work for mine."

Janice pointed a pink-tipped finger at him. "Yours is an inheritance. That's different."

"How? How am I different from a homeless man, sleeping on a bench one night, who has a big bag of money fall on him from the sky? I did nothing. I did the exact-same amount of nothing as Steve Kowalski."

Janice answered, "Again, fine. You can draw whatever conclusions you like. That is your business." She looked to Finn and then back at Rowan. "But if you just hand out money, people—unsavory people—are going to swarm around you."

She told them, "Once my friend Linsey and I were going to Sullivan Beach, and we got hungry. We stopped at McDonalds for cheeseburgers and french fries. We scarfed down the cheeseburgers right away. But then, without thinking, we took our bags of fries down to the beach. Well, this army of seagulls attacked us like nobody's business. It was awful. Like Hitchcock's-*The-Birds* awful."

Rowan looked puzzled. "Like what?"

Janice said, "Tippi Hedren?"

Finn told Rowan, "It's a movie, dude. I saw it. Pretty damn scary."

Janice continued, "Anyway, these gulls started circling over our heads. Then they started diving down at our fries, and pecking at them, and stealing them away."

The waiter appeared with a large tray bearing both their drinks and three plates of the luncheon special. After he departed, Rowan asked Janice, "So what happened with those seagulls?"

"We threw the french fries on the sand, ran back to the car, and got the hell out of there."

Rowan thought for a moment. "Okay. So, in this parable, I am *you*, and the seagulls are . . . who?"

Janice answered as if it were obvious. "The seagulls are the homeless people, Rowan. They will swarm you, and peck at you, and take everything you have if you are not careful."

Janice looked to Finn for support, but all she would say was, "That movie scared the hell out of me."

After a few bites, Janice changed the subject. "Finn, I want to say: We really appreciate you joining us on such short notice."

Finn replied, "Yeah sure. No problem."

"I read a few things about you on your website, but can you tell us more?"

"Sure. What do you want to know?"

Rowan joined in. "Are you from here in Charleston?"

"Yep. Born here; grew up here; I went to college here, too. I just didn't go for long." She pointed up the street, "I did some time at the Citadel."

Rowan said, "The military academy? I thought that was all men."

Janice told him, "No! Not for years now; many years."

Finn pointed a chip at Rowan and said, "The only reason they let me into the Citadel was they thought I was a dude. That happens to me a lot. Then they tried to change their minds, but I said the hell with that. I didn't really want to go there, but it became a matter of principle."

Rowan asked her, "What was the principle?"

Finn replied, "Hell, I don't know. It's a saying: *A matter of principle*." She continued, "I stuck it out for a year, just to be ornery. They weren't going to drive me out. But then enough was enough. I finally told my commanding officer to go fuck himself. Pardon my French, but that's what I said."

Rowan asked, "How did he react to that?"

"He kicked me out."

Janice asked her, "For telling him to you-know-what himself?"

"No. That would've made him look bad; like a pussy, you know? Like he couldn't handle a little f-bomb from a girl. So he said it was for being gay." She turned to Rowan. "I guess you weren't allowed to be gay in the military back then."

Rowan said, "Oh. So . . . Are you gay?"

Finn shrugged. "I don't know. I could be. I don't care to find out."

Janice suggested, "You could be *asexual*."

"What?"

Rowan paraphrased for Finn's benefit. "Not sexual."

"Oh. Yeah. I could be that."

Janice continued, "There's a wide spectrum of things to be now, sexually speaking. It used to be *LGB, Lesbian, Gay, Bisexual*; then they added *Transgender*, and it was *LGBT*. Now they've added *Q, I*, and *A* for *Queer, Intersex*, and *Asexual*. And some groups are lobbying to add other letters."

Rowan asked her, "What is intersex?"

Janice defined the word. "It means you have two sets of genitalia." She added, "I've read about that, but I've never seen it."

Rowan said, "Like hermaphrodites? The Bible has hermaphrodites in it."

Finn asked, "Really? In the Bible?"

"Oh yes. The Bible has eunuchs, too."

"Huh."

Janice concluded, "So maybe the *A* in *LGBTQIA* describes you. You are *asexual*; you just don't care about sex."

Finn winked at Rowan. "I don't give a fuck. Right? Again, pardon the language." She told Janice, "You know, I think I'll just tell people I'm *N*."

Janice replied, "*N*? And what does that stand for?"

"None of your business."

Janice nodded, and all three returned to eating. After a few bites,

Janice asked Finn, "About the house, can you take a mold sample from the foyer? From behind the wallboard?"

Finn answered with food in her mouth. "Sure. There's a lotta mold growin' in those houses by the water."

Janice waited for her to swallow, then added, "And I'm worried about the windows. They're too easy to break."

"Uh huh. You wanna maybe put bars on them?"

Janice scrunched up her face. "Not really. Do you think we have to?"

"Nah. It's a pretty safe area. And we might run into historical preservation bullshit." She turned to Rowan. "They don't let you do whatever you want down there. You gotta get shit approved."

Ten minutes later, the waiter appeared with the check. He leaned next to Rowan and whispered, "Did you want this, Father?"

After a puzzled moment, Finn figured out what was happening and shouted at him, "No, dude! He's not a priest!" The waiter blushed, so she added, "He just likes wearing a dress. He's a *T*; a transgender."

The waiter shifted uncomfortably as Janice reached over and took the check. She laid two twenties on it and asked Rowan, "Can you put in another twenty?"

Rowan did as she asked. Then Janice told the waiter, "That's all set."

He said, "Thank you, ma'am," and retreated quickly.

Janice stood and looked at Finn. "Sorry but I need to hit the road. I'm driving down to Savannah."

Rowan explained, "She's going to a funeral."

"Oh? Sorry to hear it."

Rowan said, "It's the funeral of a frenemy."

Finn's face contorted. "What the hell's that?"

"It's a portmanteau word."

Finn shrugged and muttered, "Whatever."

Janice stood and asked Finn, "Can you please give Rowan a ride back to the house?”

“Sure.”

“And maybe take a look at the foyer? And the windows?”

“You got it.”

“Thanks.” Janice turned to Rowan. “I’ll call you when the service is over. Make sure you have your cell phone with you.” She exited the café and crossed the street. Rowan and Finn watched her get into the Focus and speed away.

Then Rowan followed Finn out to her truck. She opened the door for him to climb up onto the seat. She grinned and told him, “This is where we see if you’re wearing underwear or going commando.” As he climbed in, she added, “Yep. You’re wearing it.”

Finn then drove back to the Battery area, stopping at its southernmost point to wag her finger at an old hotel. “They say JFK stayed there, back when he was in the Navy, back in World War Two. They say he was having sex with a Nazi spy there.”

Rowan commented, “Oh? That’s disappointing.”

“Yeah. I heard he’d have sex with anybody. Like you said, sex stuff made him do crazy shit, like banging a Nazi chick.”

Rowan directed her to take Janice’s parking spot on the side street. He pointed and said, “That’s the garden door.”

Finn asked him, “Why is it open?”

Rowan thought for a moment. “I don’t know. Maybe the wind blew it open.” Rowan jumped down from the truck, slipped under the arch, and stepped into the foliage.

Finn followed; she commented almost immediately, “Hey! There’s Saint Francis of Assisi!”

Rowan turned to her and confirmed, “Yes.” But he stopped speaking when he saw Finn’s jaw drop, and her eyes dart to a spot behind him. Rowan turned and looked, too.

Straight ahead, beneath the bench, was a dark red pool of blood. Rowan approached the pool slowly, followed by Finn. They stood together and peered over the back of the bench at the man reclining on it. He was dressed smartly in a Brooks Brothers suit, but the suit was riddled with bullet holes, and he had a large, oozing hole at his temple.

Finn broke the silence with one whispered, puzzled word: "Dude."

Rowan dropped to one knee, causing his robe to dip into the red puddle. He looked over at Finn, who had turned deathly pale, and whispered, "It's Steve Kowalski." When Finn did not react, he added, "The homeless man. He was staying here. He . . . He had a job interview this morning."

Finn spun around and leaned over a patch of thick vegetation, as if she were about to vomit. But after making a short, gagging sound, she managed to right herself and walk to the garden door. She leaned against the arch and held up her phone to Rowan, telling him hoarsely, "I'm calling the police, dude."

Rowan nodded and turned back to the body splayed out on his iron bench. He marveled that Steve Kowalski's eyes—yellowed by drugs and reddened by alcohol— were stuck in the open position. They looked up at Rowan like small, stained-glass windows.

Janice called Rowan's cell phone at five PM. He clicked it on after three rings and said, "Hello."

He heard Janice's voice. "Hey. It's me. How are things going there?"

Rowan exhaled loudly into the phone. He answered, "Not well. Not well at all. The police have the garden sealed off with tape. I'm standing outside the wall now."

Janice spoke slowly. "The police? Sealed off? Why?"

"They're investigating a murder."

"A murder! What? Who got murdered?"

"Steve Kowalski."

"The stumblebum? I'm sorry, I mean, the homeless veteran?"

"Yes. He's dead. He has been murdered."

Janice sputtered, "What? How?"

"I don't know. There are bullet holes all over, just like with Lance. That same policewoman came back, the big one. I told her how Lance had gotten murdered up in Richmond. She asked for the name of the trooper who handled Lance's case."

"His name was Dan Bateman."

"I know. She called him, and we both talked to him. He's coming here tonight to talk to you."

"To me? Where?"

"Here at the house. The policewoman said we could go back into the house, but not into the garden."

"I'll be there as fast as I can. Where's Finn?"

"She left. I think she was upset."

"Yeah, I'd think so. You get inside that house, Rowan. Don't open the door to anybody but me. Okay?"

"Okay. Why?"

"Why? Think about it."

Janice made the drive back to Savannah in a little under two hours. She parked on Battery Street and used her key to enter the front foyer. The house was dark, and very quiet. She jumped and let out a shriek when Rowan suddenly walked out of the parlor. She growled, "Agh! Rowan! You scared me."

"Sorry."

Janice stared into the parlor. "Were you sitting in the dark?"

Rowan turned back and looked. He answered, "It wasn't dark when I sat down."

"All right. Well, can we turn on some lights now?"

"Sure." Rowan crossed to the front wall and flipped two switches, lighting up both the foyer and the outside porch. He peered through the tall windows and announced, "Hey! The trooper is here. He's pulling up now."

Janice joined Rowan to watch as a *Virginia State Police* car parked in front of the house. She opened the door and waited until the driver was on the stairs before saying his name. "Trooper Bateman."

He touched his cap. "Miss Richman. Good to see you again. But I'm sorry it's under such circumstances."

Janice stepped back to allow him entrance and then guided him into the parlor. "Yes. I just got back from Laurence Myers' funeral."

"Oh? So soon?"

"It's a Jewish thing."

He removed his cap and said, "Oh. All right. I should have known that."

Janice pointed him to a love seat. Rowan followed them into the parlor, nodding gravely to the trooper. He sat in one of the two wing chairs, prompting Janice to take the other.

The trooper began right away, "Miss Richman, Rowan, I'm here to learn if there is any connection between Laurence Myers' murder and the murder of—" He pulled out his phone and dialed up a screen. "Of a Mister Steven Kowalski, on these premises, earlier today."

He continued, "I talked to a Savannah policewoman, one familiar with the case, so I'm up to speed on the facts she has gathered."

Trooper Bateman shifted uncomfortably on the seat. Then he spoke directly to Janice. "I have been pursuing several leads on Laurence Myers' case myself. I have learned some information that may indeed tie these two murders together."

Janice looked at Rowan and said, "That's a good thing. Right?"

Trooper Bateman shifted again. He answered, "Perhaps not for you, Miss Richman. Here is what I have learned: Mister Charles MacDermott hired a detective agency to monitor the activities of his partner, your father, Mister Mark Richman."

Janice was dumbfounded. She finally said, "What? When?"

"Two week ago. Apparently, Mister MacDermott has had suspicions about his partner's activities, and about his partner's drinking. The detective agency, a reputable one in Richmond, assigned people to follow your father in and around the city. And then, earlier today, an agent followed him out of the city."

The trooper paused, so Janice broke in. "They followed him . . . where exactly?"

"Here, to Charleston, Miss."

"My father? To Charleston?"

"Yes. And it gets worse. They followed him to this address in Charleston."

"No! That can't be!" Janice grabbed her phone. "I'll call him. I will talk to him right now, and we will straighten this out."

The trooper shook his head. "I have already spoken to him."

Janice set the phone down. She prompted him, "And?"

"And he said he came here to ask Mister Butler for help; to ask him to share some of his new-found wealth with his half-siblings, who were Mister Richman's clients." He checked his phone again and added, "Kitty and Ewell Butler.

"Mister Richman said he parked his car on the side of the house, by the garden door. When he got out, he saw that the garden door was open. He took a few steps inside, looked around, and spotted a dead man on a bench. Then he panicked. He ran back to his car and drove away, never realizing that he was being followed by a private detective the whole time."

Janice looked hopefully at Rowan and then the trooper. She said, "So, that proves he didn't kill him?"

The trooper allowed himself a tight smile. "Maybe. I have a statement from a private detective who says your father did not have enough time to kill anyone." He retracted the smile. "Still, the Savannah Police are calling Mister Richman a person of interest."

"How can they do that? If he has an alibi?"

"He has an alibi for himself. That doesn't rule out third-party involvement." After a moment of silence, the trooper stood and put on his cap. "And I'm afraid that's all I can say for now." He started toward the door, but he suddenly turned and asked them, "Do you two feel safe staying here tonight?"

Rowan answered, "Yes," just as Janice answered, "No."

Trooper Bateman addressed Janice. "I can call the city police, Miss Richman. I can request to have an officer assigned here."

Janice looked at Rowan and then at the trooper. "I don't know. Is that a big deal?"

He assured her, "No. You wouldn't even know someone was here. It'd probably be one officer, outside, in a patrol car."

Janice opened her mouth to say *yes* again, but Rowan overruled her. "Thank you, Trooper, but we will be all right. No one wants to murder Miss Richman. They want to murder me, and I am keeping away from all windows. I'm sitting in the dark."

The trooper gave Janice one more chance, asking, "Miss?"

She shook her head and said, "It's Mister Butler's house, so it's his decision. Thank you anyway."

The trooper touched his cap with one index finger and continued out.

Thursday

The next morning, Rowan walked out the front door by himself. His carefully measured stride took him down Church Street, in the dim light, to the White Point Garden where he stopped to watch a couple sort through a trash bin. They were a spectral sight—a grimy-looking man and an exhausted-looking woman—each appearing to be about fifty years of age.

Rowan approached them and said, "Good morning," but neither responded. He continued, "My friend tells me that there are shelters for the homeless. Do you stay in one of them?"

The man looked away, but the woman met Rowan's gaze and replied, "Shelters are too dangerous."

"Oh? Why is that?"

"They got nutty people in there. They got junkies. They got child molesters and rapists."

"Oh."

"You're safer out here on the street."

Rowan looked behind him. He said, "Or . . . You're safer at my house. You are welcome to stay at my house." He pointed up the block. "It's the one with the police tape, but that's temporary, and it's only for the garden. Come by tonight, and I'll find you a room."

The man finally spoke. He asked Rowan gruffly, "Now why would you do that?"

Rowan smiled and replied, "In my father's house there are many mansions. I go to prepare a room for you."

The man snarled, "What?"

"It's from the Bible."

"Are you the Salvation Army?"

"No."

The man turned to the woman and ordered, "That's enough here. Let's go." The woman stopped her work abruptly and fell into step behind the man, who was already moving away with grim purpose.

Rowan watched them until they disappeared. Then he walked up East Battery all the way to Waterfront Park, counting each step, before he finally circled back to the mansion. He stopped at Janice's rental car and leaned against the passenger door for fifteen minutes, watching the yellow police tape flap in the breeze.

Janice pushed open the servants' door at nine AM, carrying the Kohlmann's bag of fruit and water bottles. They idled on the street for two more minutes—with Janice texting to friends and Rowan watching the flapping tape—until Finn pulled up behind them in her Ram 250. Then both vehicles set out on the relatively short drive down I-95 to Savannah.

Janice quickly laid out their agenda to Rowan: "Okay. First, we stop at a mall and get you some more clothes. Then we visit your Savannah property."

"My third mansion."

"Yes. Then I have a stop of my own; I hope you don't mind. I need to visit my mother and grandmother, my Bubbe. It won't take long, and they live in the same place. It'll be, like, two birds with one stone. Okay?"

Rowan agreed quickly, "Okay," because he also had an addition to make. He said, "Trooper Bateman gave me some information yesterday, during our phone call."

"Oh?"

"It's Steve Kowalski's last known address, and it's just outside Savannah. I'd like to stop there."

"Okay." Janice drove for another thirty seconds before asking, "But why would we do that?"

"I have to. The man died on my property, right after meeting me. The man died in my clothes!"

"Tell me about it. Laurence died in my car."

"I know."

"I couldn't even talk to his family yesterday, I just hung out in the back like a potted plant."

Rowan shook his head. "I should have gone to that funeral service. I was connected to Lance, too, if only briefly. I am definitely connected to Steve Kowalski, and therefore to his family. This is all about obligation."

Janice agreed, "It is. In my family, that's all there is. Relentless, soul-sucking obligation." She drove for a full five minutes before she asked him, "This may sound weird but, uh, you wouldn't want to pretend you were a potential boyfriend, would you?"

"What?"

She explained, very rapidly, "It would be a *total* pretense, like a little white lie that would evaporate the second we leave. When my mother pulls me aside and asks me if you're a potential boyfriend, I could just get quiet and maybe give a little smile. That's all. You wouldn't have to do anything, and then it would be over."

Rowan thought for a moment, then replied, "I'm sorry. I don't think that's a good idea."

Janice responded immediately, "No. No, of course not. *I'm* sorry for asking. Totally . . . not professional."

Rowan puffed out his cheeks; he exhaled a short breath of air. He said, "Anyway, I think that state trooper is a real potential boyfriend."

Janice batted the suggestion away with her hand. "No way." But then she added, "What makes you think that?"

"He's so deferential when he speaks to you. He's so polite. He wants you to think well of him."

"And he wants to charge my dad with murder?"

"That too, yes."

Janice had set the GPS for a Designer Fashion Park further south on I-95. The Ford Focus and the Ram 250 pulled in there at ten-thirty AM for a quick, efficient shopping spree. This resulted in Rowan procuring two blazers, two pairs of pants, and a suit from Brooks Brothers; two pairs of shoes from Johnston and Murphy, and packs of socks and underwear from Marshalls. Finn waited outside of the first two stores, but she accompanied the others into Marshalls and purchased three cotton work shirts from a *Sale* bin.

Once back on the road, Janice returned to a discussion of the two murders. She asked, "Now, tell me, Rowan: Who would have the wherewithal to hire somebody to commit murder?"

Rowan pondered her words and replied, "*Wherewithal*? How do you mean that?"

"I mean, who would either have a gun to do it, or have the money to *hire* someone to do it."

"Hmm. Well, who comes to mind for you?"

"I would say Kitty and Ewell Butler. They have money, despite all their poor-mouthing, and they would stand to quadruple that money, quadruple it or more, if you wound up dead."

"Quintuple. Sextuple. Septuple."

"Yes."

"Octuple."

"Okay."

"So wouldn't that make them the prime suspects?"

Janice thought for a moment, then said, "For a flat-out murder, yes. But what if they made murder look like something else? Something different?"

"Like what?"

Janice raised her finger. "Well, maybe Laurence's murder was made to look like a drug buy gone bad. That's what the police think it was. Right?"

"Right. And what about Steve Kowalski's?"

"Could be that his murder was made to look like a robbery gone bad. Or that was the plan anyway. The killer broke in through the garden, supposedly to steal your stuff, but then you appeared! You surprised the burglar, and the burglar shot you dead. The police would buy that completely."

"And they wouldn't suspect Kitty and Ewell of hiring the killer?"

"Sure they would, but Kitty and Ewell would have great alibis. They would be dining at the country club with a dozen witnesses. Maybe even a priest and a rabbi."

"Then the police would have to look elsewhere. They'd have to move on to another suspect."

"Right." Janice grimaced. "Unfortunately, that could be my dad. Kitty and Ewell wouldn't hesitate to set *him* up."

Rowan considered her words. He said gently, "And the trooper implied that your father has a problem with alcohol."

Janice admitted, "He does. Before this year, he . . . drank socially. *Single malt scotch.* That's his thing. He can talk to you about distilleries in Scotland for hours. You know how some people only drink single-bean coffee, from one plantation in South America, and they know the names of all the field hands?"

"Not really."

"Well, they do, and he's like that with the whiskey makers in Scotland." Janice paused, and then claimed, "But he could always handle his drinking."

Rowan disagreed. "I don't know. The first thing I ever heard about him was from MacDermott, and it was bad. Remember? He asked you if your dad was drunk and sleeping it off somewhere. Maybe your dad thinks he's handling his drinking, but he's not; not if people are talking about him that way. And he turned up at a business meeting, with clients, clearly suffering from a hangover."

Janice raised both hands from the steering wheel and then lowered them. "Okay. Okay. Maybe you're right. Maybe that makes him an alcoholic." She added, "But it doesn't make him a murderer."

"No. Of course not."

"Of course not."

Rowan mused, "You know, if you base it on the Bible, though . . . half of us are murderers."

"What?"

"Half the members of the human race, statistically, are murderers.

There were only two people in the Garden, Cain and Abel. And one of them killed the other."

"That's depressing."

"Some things never change. No matter the year; no matter the century, or the millennium. People still kill each other. And some of them get away with it."

Janice shook her head rapidly, as if to dispel that dark thought, and said, "Well, I don't think it was my dad. Anyway, it's not my job to solve murders. Is it?" She paused, then added, "My job is to drive you to Charleston and then to Savannah, and to show you your properties."

Rowan smiled grimly. "That's turning out to be a pretty bad job, isn't it?"

Janice shook her head *no*. "I've had worse." She recalled, "I once had a job where I had to squirt people with perfume when they walked into a department store. A woman once pulled out a can of Mace and squirted me back."

Rowan laughed. "Okay. That's pretty bad. But I had a job making fruitcakes for twenty years."

"You win."

Rowan said, "I remember: We had a very old fellow at the Community named Brother Martin. It was his job to milk our one cow, which he did faithfully each day, carrying a shiny steel bucket to and from the barn. Then the cow died during a freeze, and Brother Abelard decided to switch to buying milk from a dairy. But Brother Martin still, for the remaining days of his life, carried that steel bucket out to the barn each day and then carried it back again, empty."

"Why?"

"No one knows."

"No one asked him?"

"Not to my knowledge. But how many people are like him? Doing jobs that are no longer necessary, or that even make sense?"

After a moment, Janice asked, "So . . . Were you really a fruitcake baker?"

"Yes."

"That mean little monk said you were too good for that. Too smart."

"Brother Carl?"

"Yes."

"Well, I wasn't. I pitched in when I had to. I pitched in on anything that needed to be done. I did some farming. And some hunting."

"Oh? Did you actually shoot things?"

"I did. We all did. We had a closet full of rifles, and we learned how to use them. It was either that or eat canned peaches three times a day."

"So you all carried guns?"

"No. No one *carried* a gun. Brother Abelard locked them all up. But you could access them easily, just by signing them out on a sheet."

"Why would he lock them up? I mean, if it was just you monks around?"

Rowan considered his reply. "Because sometimes Brother Abelard took in characters. Unsavory characters. They generally came for a week; maybe two. I always suspected they were running from the law. And I suspect they paid a good price to stay with us. To hide out."

Janice shuddered. "That's creepy."

"Well, most of the people *weren't* like that. Most members of the Community were good people. They were outcasts, like me; people who did not fit in anywhere else."

"So they wound up at the Community?"

"Yes."

"They would volunteer for that life? A monastic life? Work, pray, repeat?"

"Yes. Especially the Obsessive Compulsives. They wanted, they craved, *work, pray, repeat*. They wanted order, and purpose, and repetition. We got up at the same time each day, prayed at the same times, ate at the same times. Our day was orderly. And purposeful. Every day."

"It sounds awful."

"But it's exactly what some people need. It was exactly what I needed. I went in there crazy, and I came out sane."

Janice stole a look at her passenger. "Do you really think so?"

Rowan flopped out his hands, puzzled. He answered, "All I know is what I've read in my medical file. I had *an acute psychotic episode*. I was *floridly psychotic*. Maybe that's true; maybe that's what happened. Or maybe I was just overwhelmed; maybe I had just had enough."

She prodded him gently, "Enough of what?"

"Enough of being that rich kid. That prep school failure. That little bastard. Maybe I just wanted him to be gone."

Janice nodded thoughtfully, but she did not reply.

The Ford Focus and the Ram 250 pulled into Savannah at eleven forty-five. Janice turned off Oglethorpe Avenue onto Barnard Street and pointed straight ahead. She said, "Savannah is a city with many squares, Rowan. That's Orleans Square; it has a nice little fountain. My dad and I used to throw coins in it. Then my mom found out and made us stop."

"Why?"

Janice turned left. "She said it was wasteful, and I needed the money for college. Look over there. That's Chippewa Square. That's the *life's a box of chocolates* place."

"The what?"

"*Forrest Gump*?"

"What's that?"

"It's a movie. Parts were filmed here." She turned right onto Bull

Street.

Rowan said, "I do know that Savannah was founded in Seventeen Thirty-three."

"Uh oh. Here we go."

"The same day that Georgia was founded. As a colony, of course."

"Of course." Janice drove on and explained, "Anyway, here is Madison Square."

"I know."

Janice raised eyebrows. "You know?"

"Yes. I know the names of all the squares."

"Then why are you letting me babble on?"

"I want to hear how you describe them. This is your home town." She asked him, "But you didn't know the Forrest Gump thing?"

"No. Never heard of it."

"How about *Midnight in the Garden of Good and Evil*?"

"What's that?"

"A book. A movie. An abomination for the locals?"

"Nope."

Janice pulled over and turned off the ignition. She leaned forward, along with Rowan, to look up at his third and final mansion.

Though only two stories tall, the house was as deep as the combined house and garden in Charleston. Four massive columns, forty feet high, supported a stone roof set above the entranceway. Twin brick staircases, left and right, offered two separate approaches to the front door. The mustard-colored outer walls were interspersed with pairs of black shutters sitting on either side of many, many windows. A sturdy, ten-foot high wrought-iron fence circled the entire property.

Finn pulled up behind them, parked, and hopped down from the cab. Janice and Rowan got out and joined her on a slow walk around the property. After completing a full circuit, they stopped where they had begun. Janice held her arms out wide and declared, "This is even better than the Charleston house. And it is also filled with antiques."

But all Rowan would say was, "Why would it need two staircases?"

Finn offered an answer. "A lotta old houses got those. One side's for the ladies, and one side's for the gents."

"Why? Why keep them separated?"

Finn shrugged. "So they wouldn't get each other's cooties, I guess." She rubbed her thumb on the surface of the wrought iron gate. "This is starting to oxidize. You know what that means, right?"

Rowan answered, "To rust."

"Right."

Janice asked Finn, "So . . . First impression. Would you say this property needs a few, or a lot of repairs?"

Finn shook her head, causing her short brown hair to sway enough to reveal a dime-size, black onyx gauge in each earlobe. She replied, "A few. It looks to be pretty well kept-up, at least on the outside. I'll have to check the inside, of course; the plumbing and the electrical." She looked at Janice, "And the wallboards for mold."

Janice said, "Yes. Thank you."

"They're really into historical preservation down here, too. They got regulations out the wazoo. We'll have to work with someone who knows all about that."

Janice said, "I can check Hannah's List."

But Finn suggested, "I know a guy. Harry Pellettierre. He teaches at SCAD."

Rowan looked at her. "What's SCAD?"

Janice provided the answer. "The Savannah College of Art and Design. It's right over there." She pointed one block to the south, to a three-story, red-brick building. "Laurence Myers studied there. For years. He finally graduated at, like, age twenty-six."

Finn suggested, "Then maybe Harry knew him."

"Is Harry a teacher?"

"Yeah. Harry teaches interior design. He's the best. He knows all about antiques, too. He can do an appraisal if you like."

Rowan said, "Absolutely. Can you ask him to meet us for lunch?"

"Sure. Where?"

"Let him pick the place."

She told Rowan, "Okay. I'll text you the name of the restaurant, and we can all meet there." Rowan nodded, and Finn took off walking toward the college.

As he watched her go, Rowan shuddered, as if with a chill. He tensed his shoulders and narrowed his eyes. He spun around slowly, taking in a panorama view of the square.

Janice asked, "What are you doing?"

"Looking."

"Looking for what?"

"I don't know. For something bad."

"Bad? Why?"

He held up three fingers. "Because things tend to happen in threes."

Janice said, "Things like murders?"

"Yes."

Janice took a quick look around, too. Then she said, "You're right. Let's keep moving. I need to visit Mom and Bubbe or they'll have a conniption. It won't take long."

"Where do they live?"

"About fifteen blocks from here, at Forsyth Park. It's where I used to live."

"Oh? Until when?"

"Until I moved to Richmond a year ago. That's when Bubbe took over my room." Janice added, "She has memory issues."

They got back into the car and drove south to a four-story apartment building composed of sand-colored bricks. Janice pulled over on the park side of the entrance and led Rowan under a black canopy imprinted with the words: *Park Place*. Directly inside the door, an elderly security guard looked up from his seat at a desk.

Janice said, "I'm here to see my mother."

"Who's that?"

"Missus Richman. Cora Richman."

The guard's lip seemed to twitch upward and then stop. He reached under the desk with his right hand, pressed a button, and then raised the same hand to point to an elevator. "Enjoy your visit, Miss."

"Thank you."

Janice and Rowan rode up to the second floor, exited, and turned right. Janice dug out a key as they walked down a short hallway. As she stuck the key in a door, she turned to Rowan. "You look worried, Rowan. Don't be. My mother and Bubbe won't bite."

Rowan assured her, "I'm not worried about your mother. And I'm certainly not worried about anyone named *Bubbe*."

Janice opened the door onto a sumptuously decorated living room, featuring a bay window with a park view. A short woman in a black dress and white apron emerged from the kitchen to the right. She feigned surprise. "Janice! Imagine seeing you here!"

"I was in town on business, Mom."

"Ah. Business. From the big city of Richmond?" She looked Janice up and down and commented, "You look so pretty in the pink—the lips, the nails."

"Thank you."

The woman then pointed over Janice's shoulder and asked, "And who is this well-dressed young man? A suitor?"

Janice assured Rowan. "She's kidding; she does this to annoy me." She told her mother, "This is Rowan James Butler, a client of the firm. I'm helping him get set up here in Savannah."

Janice's mother extended a hand and Rowan shook it. She said, "I'm Cora. Just call me that. I don't like to use Richman." She looked back at Janice. "Can you blame me?"

Janice looked at Rowan and rolled her eyes as a second black-clad woman emerged, this one holding a wooden salad bowl and a dishtowel. Janice said, "And this is Bubbe. Bubbe, this is Rowan."

The second woman—a slightly older, slightly shorter version of Cora—also shook hands with Rowan. She said, "Did I hear you were a suitor?"

Janice replied, "No, you did not, Bubbe. He's a client."

"Maybe someone said you were wearing a suit?"

Janice assured her, "No."

"But he is wearing a suit."

"He is. Yes."

"Well, can you stay for lunch? We just finished, but I can pull it all out again. It's no trouble."

Janice said, "No. I thought we could just sit and visit for a few minutes. Then I have to get Rowan to a meeting."

Cora stepped back and pointed to a leather sofa near the window. "Well, a meeting. Yes. Come sit here, Rowan. You can see the park best from this sofa."

Rowan said, "Thank you," and sat where directed. Janice followed, sitting at the opposite end of the long couch.

Cora smiled and asked her, "What? Does he have germs?" She pointed her mother toward the kitchen, "Bubbe, can you make some tea?"

Janice protested, "Mom, we really don't have time."

"For tea?"

"Not the way Bubbe makes it. No offense, Bubbe."

The old woman asked, "What? I take too long?"

"No, just, for now, it would be too long."

Janice's grandmother decided, "I'll make it. If you're still here, you'll drink it. If not, we'll drink it."

She slipped back into the kitchen as Cora sat in a leather chair, inclined her head toward Rowan, and whispered, "She'll probably forget why she went into the kitchen. Her memory is gone. Her short-term memory, anyway. She can tell you anything you want about John. F. Kennedy and Marilyn Monroe. Or Eddie Fisher and

Elizabeth Taylor.”

Rowan nodded sympathetically. Cora then raised her voice and asked Janice, “So, are you still seeing that young attorney?”

“No, Mom.”

“Why?”

“Because he was married.”

“Oh no! How did you find that out?”

“I ran into him at the courthouse, and he had a wedding ring on.”

“What a rat.” She turned to include Rowan. “Do you know who else turned out to be a rat? Her father. Do you know Mister Mark Richman, Esquire?”

Rowan admitted, “Yes. I’ve met him.”

“He’s a rat. And he’s a drunk, too.”

Janice protested, “Mom!”

“What?”

“This is not an appropriate topic.”

“What? Now I’m not appropriate?”

“The *topic* is not appropriate. It’s not something to discuss with a . . . virtual stranger.”

“You said he was a client.”

“Then not with a client! He barely knows Dad. He doesn’t want to hear all these bad things about him.”

Cora retreated slightly, clamping her mouth closed as the three of them listened to Bubbe clattering pans in the kitchen. Cora finally broke the silence by pointing to Janice and smiling. “But! Mark Richman gave me what I wanted—my little girl here. My jew-el.”

Janice threw up her hands in exasperation. She accused her mother, “Seriously? Did you just put the accent on *jew*?”

“No. What? What do you mean?”

“It’s *jool*, one syllable; not *jew-el*.”

“I’m sorry. That’s the way I say it. What’s wrong with that?”

“It’s not how you pronounce the word.”

“Okay. But Rowan does know we’re Jews, right?”

"Yes!"

Cora turned to her guest and changed the subject, asking amiably, "So . . . How are you liking our city of Savannah, Rowan?"

Janice grumbled, "He's been here for one hour, Mom."

Cora told him, "It's very well-organized, Rowan. With the grids and the squares. You'll like that."

Surprisingly, Rowan shook his head *no*. He replied, "The Bible warns against things becoming too organized."

"The Bible?"

"Yes. In *First Chronicles*, Satan tricks King David into getting too organized; into numbering all his subjects, even though God has said not to do that. David falls for the trick, and he pays a huge price with years of famine."

Cora blinked and replied, "King David. Yes."

Rowan pointed out, "In the Christian Bible, *Chronicles* is divided into *First* and *Second Chronicles*. In the Hebrew Bible, though, it's all one book."

"It's in the Hebrew Bible?"

"Yes."

Cora admitted, "I did not know that." And she looked at Janice.

Janice admitted, "I didn't know we had a bible."

After a few more minutes of awkward talk, Janice rose from the couch and took a large, sideways step toward the door. This prompted Rowan to get up, too, followed by Cora. Janice continued to sidle toward the exit while Rowan looked into the kitchen and called, "It was nice to meet you, Bubbe."

Janice's grandmother called back, "What? You're not staying for tea?"

"It doesn't look like it. I wish we could."

Cora pulled Janice aside. "Is he gay? Like that Laurence boy was?"

Janice kissed her mother on the cheek. "No. He's just not interested. It happens."

"It happens to you too much."

"Thank you for that."

"Oh? Now the sarcasm starts?"

Janice ducked into the kitchen and kissed her grandmother goodbye, too, adding, "We'll take a rain check on the tea, Bubbe. I promise."

Janice then opened the door and led Rowan into the hallway. He waved to both ladies and called, "Goodbye." At the elevator, he whispered to Janice, "Is Bubbe offended that we didn't drink the tea?"

Janice assured him, "No. By now, she's forgotten we were even there."

Back in the car, Rowan scrolled through his I-phone until he found the address for Steve Kowalski. He read it aloud as Janice keyed the information into the GPS console. Then they drove up the interstate, for six miles, to the Garden City exit.

Their destination, the Peach Tree Motel, was visible from the highway via a sputtering neon sign. The Peach Tree was a long and low motel, one story high, with twenty rooms radiating out in each direction from a main office.

Janice said, "I can tell from here, this place is full of mold spores."

Rowan replied, "Mold again?"

"Yes."

"Are you allergic to other things, too?"

"Yes. Cockroach feces. I'm betting they have an alarming amount of cockroach feces here, too."

Rowan checked his phone and said, "The room number is *one-twelve*." Janice spotted the number near the westernmost end and pulled the Ford Focus into a space by the door. Rowan led the way up and knocked quietly. After a few seconds, he knocked with more force, eliciting the response, "Get the fuck out of here! Whoever you are!"

It was a woman's voice, so Rowan responded, "Missus Kowalski?"

After a pause, the woman demanded, "Who wants to know?"

"My name is Rowan Butler. I knew your husband Steve. Will you open the door and talk to me?"

"Are you alone?"

"No. My . . . " He turned to Janice, "What are you exactly?"

"I'm . . . an employee of your law firm."

The woman heard her and snarled, "Law firm?"

Rowan assured her, "The law firm part is irrelevant."

"What?"

"It's not why I'm here."

After another pause, the woman asked, in a lower voice, "Let me put it this way: Is it gonna help me or hurt me to open this door?"

Rowan assured her again, "It's going to help you."

The door opened slowly revealing a short, skinny woman, with bright yellow hair, holding a long-barrel handgun. Janice gasped, but Rowan remained calm. He asked, "May we come in and talk?"

The woman's eyes shot from Rowan to Janice and back again. She finally pulled back, lowered the gun, and said, "You can come in, but you'd better not be lying to me about who you are. I hate lying."

Rowan answered, "So do I." He stepped into a rectangular room with two single beds. Strips of torn wallpaper curled outward from its walls, which were undecorated except for a garish poster of a rock group. Janice followed him in, but she left the door open as an escape route.

Rowan asked, "*Are* you Missus Kowalski?"

"I'm Kat. Who the fuck are you?"

"I'm Rowan. And that's Janice Richman."

The woman asked Janice, "Are you a lawyer?"

Janice was covering her nose with her hand. She lowered it to answer, "No."

Kat Kowalski made a series of tight circles with the handgun. "Then what's this crap about a law firm?"

"Well—"

"Are you from the high school?"

Janice and Rowan both answered, "No."

"Do you work for that counselor son of a bitch? That Mister T son of a bitch?"

Rowan held up both hands. "No. I don't even know who that is."

"You better *find out* who he is. From what I hear he's some kind of kinky creep. Some sex pervert." Kat set the gun down on the nearer bed and said, "I take good care of my kid! I drive him to school. To the front door anyway. That's *my* part! Keeping him inside is your part!"

Rowan insisted, "We're not from a school."

"You shouldn't be bothering me. Not today. My fucking husband just died!"

Rowan said, "We know. And we're sorry." After a pause, he added, "Missus Kowalski—"

"Kat!"

"Kat. Your husband slept at my house two nights ago. He died in my garden, wearing my clothes."

Kat stared at Rowan; then she asked, "What is this? Some kind of weird sex thing?"

"No!"

"Was he doing you for money?"

"No! No, he was looking for a job in Charleston. As a mechanic."

"Charleston? How the hell did he get up there? I got the car."

Rowan admitted, "I don't know."

"Probably hitch-hiked, but I don't know who'd pick him up. Unless it was some sex pervert."

Janice's nose was now running, and her eyes were starting to close. She told Rowan, "I need some help here. The mold is getting to me."

Rowan asked, "What can I do?"

Janice appealed directly to Kat. "I always bring tissues, but today, I grabbed the wrong purse. Please, do you have any?"

Kat answered, "Tissues? Does this look like the fucking Ritz? We got one roll of toilet paper. You can use some if you want."

Janice stared at the bathroom door in alarm, but she replied, "Thank you," and hurried toward it. She pulled open the door, stepped in, and let out a shriek.

A teenage boy was standing in the tub, fully dressed, his large head framed against an open window. He was holding a steak knife in his right hand and a metal fork in his left. He was tall, like Steve Kowalski, with a flat buzz cut and swatches of acne across both cheeks.

Kat turned at the sound and peered through the door. She shouted at the boy, "Bo! Put those down." The boy obeyed, and she followed up with, "How the fuck did you get in the bathroom?"

"I climbed through the window."

"Why was the window open?"

"I unlocked it this morning, in case I needed to break in."

"You need to get your ass back to school."

The boy glared at Janice and Rowan. "Who are they? Are they from the school?"

Rowan shook his head *no*. Janice did, too, as she reached slowly to her left and pawed at the toilet paper roll.

Kat snapped, "Get your ass out here, Bo!" The boy stepped over the tub rim, squeezed past Janice, and joined his mother. Kat added, "And put those things down." The boy laid the knife and fork down on the bed, next to the handgun. "Is that office counselor fucking with you again?"

Bo mumbled, "No. I didn't go the office today. I didn't go to school at all."

Janice stood in the bathroom and blew her nose several times. She tossed the papers into the toilet and flushed. Then she unrolled three more feet of toilet paper and folded it up. She walked out past Rowan, muttering, "I'm sorry. I have to get out of here. I need air," and exited the room.

Rowan looked from Kat to Bo wondering what to say. Kat took the initiative. "So, Rowan Butler, how are you going to help us exactly? Are you going to give us money?"

Rowan shot a furtive look at the door. "Well, no. I can't just *give* you money, can I?"

"Sure you can. People do." Kat then conceded, "But they usually want something in return."

"Yes. I suppose we all need money."

"We sure fucking do."

"Well . . . What do you do for money now?"

"I clean houses." She inclined her head toward the bathroom. "I mop out toilets, scrub kitchen floors, that kinda stuff."

"I see. Well . . . I suppose, you could do that for *me*. In exchange for money."

Kat considered the offer. She replied, "Yeah? Where?"

Rowan dug out his phone, pulled up his address, and showed it to her. She got out her own phone and took a picture of Rowan's screen. She said, "All right. I got it. How much would you pay?"

"How much? Let's see. I can offer you a hundred dollars a day, assuming the ATM lets me. And I can offer you board as well."

"A board? What do I want with a fucking board?"

"No. Board."

"What is that?"

"It means a free place to stay."

"No rent?"

"No."

Kat snapped her fingers at Bo and pointed to a chest of drawers. "Pack up, Bo. Now!" She turned to Rowan. "It is *now*, right? Today? Or do you want us to come tomorrow?"

Rowan answered, "You can come today if you like, but wait a few hours. We have a lunch to go to; then we'll be at the house to let you in."

"You'll let me in to . . . clean stuff?"

"Yes."

"How much stuff?"

Rowan shrugged. "I honestly don't know. I haven't been inside." He noticed her wary look and elaborated, "I just got the house. I walked around it this morning, and looked at it, but that's all."

"Okay. How big is it?"

"It's big. It's really more of a mansion."

"Uh huh. How many bathrooms?"

"I have no idea. More than one. That's for sure."

Kat mulled this new information. She told Rowan, "We may have to re-negotiate a price after I see the place."

Rowan was quick to agree. "Sure. Okay." He backed toward the door. He stopped to tell Bo, "I'm very sorry about your father." He turned to Kat, "And about your husband." He gestured at the shabby room, "I know it must be . . . a bad situation."

Kat replied, "Yeah, well, it ain't good, is it?"

"No. Of course not. Have you made funeral arrangements?"

"Fuck no. I don't know where to start with that. Steve was a veteran, but that ain't worth shit."

Rowan corrected her. "That's not entirely true. I was just reading about my father's funeral in his papers. He enlisted in the Army Reserve at age nineteen, which was news to me. He never saw combat, or even left the country, but he *did* get an honorable discharge at age twenty-five. That entitled him to three hundred dollars for a funeral, and to another three hundred for a burial plot."

Kat crinkled her nose. "And, like I said, that ain't shit."

"No?"

"No. When we buried Steve's mom it cost us a grand just for the fucking coffin." She shook her head. "Six hundred bucks? That's a cheap cremation and a little fucking keepsake box. Like you'd get for a dog.”

Rowan thought for a moment, then said, “I also read in those papers that I own a family plot at the Oakwood Cemetery in Richmond. It has room for many more graves. Steve can have one.”

Kat pondered Rowan’s latest offer. She shook her head at him suspiciously and said, “Let’s not worry about that for now. I sure ain’t. We’ll pack up here, and we’ll see you at that address tonight.” She hiked her thumb toward the door, indicating that Rowan should leave. He made a respectful half-bow and backed out.

Janice was standing outside by the car, still blowing her nose. Rowan opened the passenger door, so she stuffed the toilet paper into her purse and climbed in. Rowan accessed a text from Finn with the name and address of a restaurant. He read it aloud, “The Blue Pub, One-eleven Bull Street, Savannah.” Janice punched in the information on the GPS and pulled away from the Peach Tree Motel.

She moaned, “Agh! My God! That motel was so disgusting.”

“That’s why they need to get out of it.”

Janice paused to let his words sink in; then she replied, “Oh no, Rowan. No! You didn’t.”

“What? I invited them to the Savannah house, *but* they are going to be working. Earning their keep.” He added, “Cleaning toilets and stuff.”

Janice banged the steering wheel and shook her head, but she did not reply. They covered the distance to the Blue Pub quickly and parked across the street from the entrance. Before he opened the door, Rowan told Janice, “Hold on. I want to look around.” He swiveled so that he could see up and down the side street. Then he said, “Okay. It’s clear,” and got out.

Finn was waiting outside the pub, standing next to a handsome, nattily dressed gentleman. As Janice and Rowan approached, she introduced him. “This is Harry. He’s the designer I was telling you about.”

Up close, Harry looked even better. Every item in his attire—

which included a two-piece linen suit, a maroon pocket square, a yellow silk tie with diamond stickpin, and polished wingtip shoes—suggested a high-fashion sense. Janice spoke to him in awe, "Sir, you look so nice."

The man laughed easily, as if used to deflecting compliments. He told her, "Not as nice as you, my dear."

Janice blushed and stammered, "I don't know about that." She pointed to herself and then to her companion. "I'm Janice, and this is Rowan."

The man extended his hand to her and then to Rowan, saying, "Harry Pellettierre, Janice. Harry Pellettierre, Rowan. That's spelled with two *L*s, two *T*s, and two *R*s."

Rowan asked, "Is that French?"

"Yes."

"And what does it mean?"

Harry answered, "It means *dealer in pelts*." He quickly added, "Though I wouldn't be caught dead in a pelt. I'm faux fur all the way." He turned to include Finn and asked, "Shall we lunch?" He turned and walked toward the entrance of the pub, pointing a manicured index finger at a blue sign bearing the words: *Everton FC*.

Janice asked Harry, "What is Everton FC?"

Before he could answer, a stocky, black-haired man in a blue apron, stepped through the open door. The man told Harry, in a Merseyside accent, "Lovely to see you, sir. As always." Then he looked at Janice. "Everton FC, Miss, is an English football club from the city of Liverpool."

Janice smiled and answered, "Ah."

Harry led the way to a high-top table near the back, pointing out other blue memorabilia along the way. He inquired of the group, "Is this table all right?" and the three nodded their assent.

The black-haired man arrived at the table carrying menus. He introduced himself to the newcomers, "I'm Jack Stokes, proprietor of this pub."

Harry added, "And an avid soccer-slash-football fan."

Jack Stokes conceded, "It's soccer over here, sir. I've given up on that one."

Harry urged him, "Explain the décor, Jack, if you would."

"Certainly, sir. I am an Everton fan, and their signature color is this blue."

Janice said, "It is a beautiful shade of blue."

"Thank you, Miss. I think so, too. And the décor indicates that this is a blue pub, as opposed to a red pub. Red is the signature color of the *other* team from my hometown, Liverpool FC. If you're an Everton fan, decked out in your blue, you wouldn't want to walk into a red pub. And vice versa."

Janice asked, "So . . . Is there a red pub in Savannah?"

He answered, "No. But there *could be*, Miss. Those bloody Liverpool fans are everywhere." He looked to Harry, as if for permission, "May I put in a quick word about the travel service?"

Harry smiled. "Please do."

"I am also the proprietor of Jack Stokes Merseyside Travel. I run it right here, out of the pub. We'll take you across the pond to the best football matches in Liverpool and Manchester." He looked to Janice, "And, Miss, if you prefer, we'll run you up to Bronte country—*Jane Eyre*, *Wuthering Heights*, all that."

Janice smiled politely, but did not respond.

Jack Stokes then proceeded to take drink orders from the group, talking them into a round of Merseyside Ales. Finn and Rowan then ordered cheeseburger baskets, while Janice and Harry opted for grilled-chicken salads.

Once the proprietor had departed, Harry took it upon himself to open the conversation. "I have a joke to share with you all. It's a geography joke, and there aren't very many of those in the world, so I hope you like it. Finn and I worked this out one day while re-designing a drawing room."

Finn said, "You mean *you* worked it out."

Harry went on, "We discovered—and I swear this is true—that Finn and I each have an Aunt Mathilda."

"Yeah, but mine's a great aunt."

"Correct. So between us, we have a Greater Aunt Tillie and a Lesser Aunt Tillie."

Harry paused and looked to Rowan and Janice to respond. When they did not, he admitted to Finn, "I guess you're right. It's just not funny."

Finn said, "No. It's not. And I still don't get it."

"They are island groups! The Antilles. The Greater and the Lesser Antilles."

"If you say so."

"They are part of the archipelago stretching from Florida to Venezuela."

"If you say so."

A young waitress appeared at the table, set down four pints of ale, and slipped silently away.

Harry shook his head back and forth rapidly. "All right. So my attempt at humor has failed miserably. Please allow me one more try."

Rowan smiled and replied, "Sure."

Harry looked from face to face, then said, "I do an icebreaker activity with my new art students that I call *thumbnail sketches*. These are short statements that tell you all you need to know about a particular person. As a rule, a thumbnail sketch always begins with the words: *He is the type of person who*."

Harry stopped here to check their understanding, and their level of interest. When satisfied, he continued. "I'll go first. Here is a thumbnail sketch of my department head: *He is the type of person who will stop speaking to you in mid-sentence if someone more important comes along*."

Janice smiled. "Yes, I know that guy."

Harry smiled back tightly. "We all do." He looked at Finn. "Of course, you could also begin with *she*, as in: *She's the type of person who.*"

Finn asked, "Who . . . what?"

"You tell me. You finish it."

Finn thought for a moment. "Okay. I think I got it. Here goes: *She's the type of person who will tell you she wants marble for her backsplash and then swear she didn't say that; that she really said quartz; and then make you switch it out and pay for it yourself.*"

Harry assured her, "All right. That's good. Wordy, but good."

Janice raised up a finger to indicate she would go next. "Here's one: *He's the type of person who would say he wants to get married, but fail to mention that it's not to you. It's to the girl who just dumped him, right before he met you.*"

Harry said, "Good. Sad, but good."

He turned to Rowan, who complied with, "All right. Here's mine: *He's the type of person who would call your mother his client, when she was really, perhaps, his lover.*"

Harry paused. "All right. Good. Somewhat Oedipal, but good."

At that moment, Jack Stokes and the young waitress delivered two baskets and two salad plates to the table, and the group began to eat. After several quiet bites, Janice asked Harry, "Did you, by any chance, know a student named Laurence Myers? He graduated from SCAD."

"I don't think so. What did he major in?"

"I'm not sure. He changed majors several times."

"I see. Well, what line of work did he go into?"

"He was a dresser for a TV station. And he owned a salon."

Harry winked at Rowan and answered, "And you think I would know him?"

Janice shrugged. "You might."

"Because you think every gay man knows every other gay man?"

Janice protested, "No!"

He smiled. "Admit it. You do think that."

Janice smiled back. "Okay. Well, maybe every one here in Savannah."

"Oh? Do you know every straight man here?"

Janice shrugged. "If they're Jewish and single? Possibly. Anyway, Laurence Myers died this week."

Harry grimaced. "Oh no."

Rowan added, "He was murdered up in Richmond, outside the Virginia Squire. It's a bar frequented by homosexuals."

"Yes, I know the establishment." Harry winked at Finn this time but spoke to Rowan. "*Homosexual* is an awfully long word, Rowan. Five syllables in length. Don't you think *gay* is more economical?"

Rowan replied, "It's sesquipedalian."

"Pardon?"

"Sesquipedalian means a word with many syllables."

"Yes. It is that."

Rowan frowned and asked him, "Is *homosexual* an offensive term?"

"No. It's just dated. And who wants to sound dated?"

"So I should switch to *gay*?"

Harry smiled broadly at Finn and said, "Well, that would be a personal decision."

Finn warned him, "Don't you start, Harry."

After a moment, Rowan said, "We had homosexuals, I mean gays, in the Community."

It was Finn who asked, "What's the Community?"

"The place where I lived; the place where I was a monk."

Harry asked, "You were a monk?" Rowan nodded, and Harry went on, "I think it's fair to say that every community has its share of gays—from the clergy, to the government, to the military. I hear they have even infiltrated the world of interior design."

Finn said, "The military's got 'em big time."

Harry told her, "Yes. From those Joint Chiefs of Staff on down. Seriously? *Joint*? St*aff*?"

Rowan said, "There are lots of gays in the clergy."

Harry smiled briefly and answered, "Tell me about it. I was an altar boy."

Finn registered surprise. She asked him, "Where?"

"Right here, in Catholic Savannah."

Janice pointed to Rowan and announced, "Well, not only was this guy a monk, he was a celibate one."

Rowan affirmed, "That's true."

Harry asked him, "How long ago was that?"

"What's today?"

"Thursday."

"Then it has been four days."

"Oh? Well, assuming nothing has happened in the last four days, does that mean you have never . . . indulged?"

Rowan asked him, "Indulged?"

"Engaged in . . . sexual intercourse. Of any variety."

Rowan admitted, "No. Never."

"Isn't that unusual?"

Finn rolled her eyes. "Here we go."

Harry protested, "What?"

"The sex talk, Harry. It always comes back to it. Rowan and me don't want to talk about sex. All right? We got other things on our minds."

Rowan shrugged. "I don't mind talking about it. It might be instructive." He told Harry, "There was a famous monk named Thomas Aquinas who never, as you say, indulged."

Janice pointed to Rowan again. "And *Thomas* was Rowan's monk name."

"Yes. It was."

Harry asked him, "Were you named for that famously celibate fellow?"

"No. I was named for Thomas the Apostle. Doubting Thomas." He reflected for a moment, then added, "I had my doubts, right from the beginning."

Harry said, "Thomas Aquinas has several high schools named after him."

Rowan expanded on the story. "Thomas's brothers once hired a prostitute to seduce him, but instead of *indulging*, he drove the prostitute away with a burning stick."

Harry deadpanned, "Several very dull high schools."

"That night two angels appeared to Thomas as he slept; this strengthened his determination to remain celibate for his entire life."

Harry asked, "And did he?"

"Yes."

"Like you."

"Yes."

Janice interjected, "Though a nun tried to seduce him."

This comment received a look of disapproval from Rowan, and he did not reply. Harry said, "A nun? That must have been awkward. One might expect such behavior from a priest, but a nun?"

Jack Stokes appeared at tableside and inquired, "Will there be anything else, folks?"

Harry replied, "Just the check," and Jack Stokes produced it immediately in his hand, like a magician with a quarter. Janice snatched it away, though, announcing, "Lunch will be paid for by the Law Offices of MacDermott and Richman."

After the bill was settled, Harry led the group back out into the sunshine where they split up into pairs. Janice and Rowan crossed the street to the Ford Focus; Finn led Harry to the Ram 250.

They arrived, just seconds apart, at Rowan's Savannah property. Rowan again showed great caution getting out of the car, turning three-hundred-sixty degrees to scan the square and its surrounding streets.

Finn jumped down from her truck, hit the ground, and yelled over to her companion. "Settle a bet here, Harry. Why are there two staircases on this house?"

He answered as if it were obvious. "One is for ladies, and one is for gentlemen."

Finn pointed to Rowan and Janice. "See! I told you. It was cooties!"

Harry added, "These staircases are a nod to a more virtuous time. A gentleman would not ascend the stairs behind a lady and ogle her ankles, or her derriere, or anything else."

The two men and two women divided and climbed the separate staircases. When they met at the top, Rowan stopped and looked from Harry to Finn. He told them solemnly, "Listen: There is something you need to know before we go any further. Something very important."

Finn looked at him expectantly; Harry said, "Do tell."

Rowan continued, "It's something Janice and I *should have* told you earlier, but . . . we're still working it out ourselves."

Finn took a step closer; Harry's eyes opened wide. He said, "We are all ears."

Rowan told them, "On Monday, I got what I guess you would call some good news. My late parents had left me three properties. Three mansions, really, and some other monies."

Harry looked up at the imposing columns. "You own three of these palaces?"

Rowan admitted, "Yes."

Finn muttered, "Yeah, that's some good news all right."

He told her, "Yes. But, as you saw for yourself up in Charleston, that news has come at a terrible price." Rowan turned to Harry. "Since Monday, two people—two people who we knew—have been murdered."

Harry gulped. "Good heavens."

Rowan's voice dropped. "They were standing and talking to us, just like you are now, and then . . . ."

He trailed off, and Janice completed the thought. "They were murdered, in cold blood." She told Harry, "One was that Laurence

Myers that I asked you about, from SCAD. Finn knows who the other guy was, because she was there to find him in Rowan's garden."

Rowan took back the narration. "We think each man was killed because he was mistaken for me."

Harry said, "You?"

"Yes. That's our working theory, anyway."

Janice spoke up. "What Rowan saying is that we—and *we* now includes you two—you may all be in danger."

Rowan nodded.

Finn and Harry exchanged a look; then Finn replied, "Well, here's my working theory, whatever that is: It sounds like only *men* are getting killed, and I need the money, so I'm still in."

Harry added, "So am I! No question about it."

Janice asked him, "You're not afraid?"

"Are you asking that because I'm gay?"

Janice protested, "No!"

Harry informed her, "I'm gay, and I'm brave. Sometimes heroically so." He hiked up his right pant leg to reveal a tan leather holster and the butt of a small handgun. "I am licensed to carry and use this, and I have done so as recently as two months ago. In Atlanta."

Even Finn seemed impressed at these revelations. "Harry! You shot somebody in Atlanta?"

He replied, "No, but I was ready to. I drew down on a mugger with a steady, two-handed aim, fully prepared to squeeze the trigger, when he turned tail and ran."

Finn replied, "Well! Good for you!" She looked down at his ankle. "Man, I gotta get me one of those."

Harry assured her, "It was the best seventy-five dollars I've ever spent."

"Yeah? That's all it cost?"

"That's all the permit cost. The gun and holster were expensive, but I wanted good ones."

"How much?"

"Believe me: You don't want to know."

Rowan looked at Janice. He raised his eyebrows and concluded, "Okay. So . . . everybody has been warned, and everybody is still in?"

Harry answered, "Absolutely; positively," and Finn added, "Yeah. What he said."

Janice unlocked the ornate wooden door and walked in. They all paused before a mahogany-and-gold staircase. Rowan asked Harry and Finn, "Where would you like to start?"

Harry pointed into a parlor on the left and answered for them. "That's as good a place as any," and he led the way in.

After a quick look around the room, he commented, "There are some very fine pieces here, Rowan, but they are just that—pieces. There is no controlling color palate; there is no editorial point of view. This room does not say: *I am honoring the burnt-umber beauty of Siena*. No. This room says: *I bought a lot of expensive things in Italy, and I am storing them here*."

Finn poked Rowan and said, "See? I told you he was good."

Harry continued, "And this wallpaper. It's so florid. It borders on the psychotic."

Rowan answered, very seriously, "That's what they called me at the hospital."

"Pardon me?"

"In the report from the psychiatric hospital. They used that term: *The patient is floridly psychotic*."

"Really? I thought I had coined it."

"No. And I must say, Harry: I like the wallpaper."

Harry raised his hands in mock-surrender, muttering, *"Droit de seigneur."*

This prompted a "Huh?" from Finn.

He defined it as, *"The right of the lord*. Though it usually applies to sex."

Finn warned him, "Don't start."

As the group moved out of the parlor, they heard footsteps outside. Rowan peered through the glass. Then he opened the front door, revealing the short, wiry figure of Kat Kowalski. She was holding a large black suitcase in her left hand and a bucket of cleaning supplies in her right. She called over her shoulder to her son, "Bo! This is the place. Get outta the fucking car!"

Bo emerged from the passenger side of a vintage brown-and-yellow Ford. He carried a matching black suitcase in his left hand, and he clutched the rolled-up rock band poster from the motel room under his arm.

Kat looked over Rowan's shoulder. She asked him, "Who are these people? Do they live here?"

Rowan took a step back. He pointed and said, "Well, you have met Janice. This is Finn, and this is Harry."

Harry waved politely; Finn just glared.

Kat said, "If they live here, we gotta re-negotiate some more."

Rowan assured her, "They don't live here. They will be working here." He added, for Janice's sake, "Just like you."

Bo joined his mother, prompting Harry to point past him and ask, "Is that a Nineteen Sixty-four Galaxie?"

Bo grunted, "Yeah."

Harry looked at Finn. "They call it THE classic muscle car."

Kat replied, "I call it a piece of shit. Do you wanna buy it?"

Harry swallowed. "Uh, no."

Rowan told the new arrivals, "Harry is taking us on a design tour. You two are welcome to join us."

Kat asked, "What for?"

"You might find it interesting."

Kat assured him, "Not a chance."

"Oh. Okay."

"I'm not gonna lie to you. I hate lying."

"I know."

"So, where can we stash our stuff?"

"Well," Rowan pivoted and pointed up the staircase. "Up there, the first two bedrooms on the left. You can take your pick."

Bo started up the stairs; Kat complained, "What? We're both in the same room? What is this, the Peach Tree Motel?"

Rowan explained, "No. No! You should *each* pick a room."

Janice, who had been struggling to remain quiet, blurted out, "Rowan!"

"What?"

"This is your house cleaner? And her kid?"

"Yes."

"And you're giving them the master bedroom? And another room?"

Rowan told her, "They need their own rooms. They need privacy. Believe me, I know about lack of privacy."

Janice stepped back and made a show of closing her mouth.

Thirty minutes later, after touring all the rooms downstairs and the unoccupied ones upstairs, Finn and Harry prepared to leave.

Finn jiggled the front door knob. She told Rowan, "You got some structural issues here, but nothing major. I can turn and burn on them jobs early next week. Then Harry can follow up and fix everything that I fucked up. Pardon my French. Sound good?"

Rowan replied, "Yes, that sounds good."

Janice said, "As for payment: Please fax me an itemized list of the jobs, with prices."

Finn winked at Rowan. "Yes, ma'am. We'll stick it to the Law Offices of Whoever and Whatever."

Janice's face turned white.

Finn smiled. "Hey, I'm just messing with you. We always provide an estimate before we start. Harry will send his to me, and I will collate them for ya'll."

Janice said, "Thank you." She and Rowan walked out onto the porch and watched Finn and Harry pull away in the Ram 250. Janice asked Rowan, "Now that you've seen both places, have you decided where you want to live?"

"What do you mean?"

"Charleston or Savannah? You have to choose one."

He told her, adamantly, "No, I don't have to choose one. I can choose both. It's like the Toyota Corolla and the Ford Ranger. They're different vehicles, with different purposes. The best choice is to keep both."

Janice replied wonderingly, "You're keeping *both*?"

Rowan nodded.

Janice shrugged and said, "Okay. Shall I tell Mister MacDermott that?"

"No, I'll tell him. Tomorrow. Can you set up a meeting for us all? Just like the meeting on Monday?"

"With the half-siblings?"

"Yes. And the lawyers."

"Sure."

"And can you get me that big laptop?"

"The laptop? For Doctor Bresnahan?"

"No."

Janice waited for further explanation, but none was forthcoming. She finally said, "I'll take care of it." She pointed back inside. "And what about the Kowalskis?"

"What about them?"

"You can't just leave them here tomorrow."

"I can. They'll be cleaning the place."

"Rowan! They could be cleaning the place out! All of your antiques! They could steal them and . . . fence them, or whatever it is they do."

"I don't believe they would do that."

"You're too trusting! You don't think somebody would *steal* from you? Rowan? Remember: Somebody is trying to *kill* you."

"I know." He added, "But it's not the Kowalskis."

Janice scanned the dark square across the street. She said, "No, but it's somebody." Then she repeated his own words back to him, "And things come in threes."

Friday

Early the next morning, Janice and Rowan took off on the longest leg of their journey, the drive from southern Georgia to northern Virginia.

Once back on I-95, Janice glanced over at Rowan, did a double-take, and said, "You do love that iPhone! What are you up to now?"

"I'm communicating."

"With whom?"

"With . . . the Internet."

"Come on! You're stalling again. With whom on the Internet?"

"Dan Bateman."

"Trooper Bateman! Why?"

"I told you, I'm interested in the process."

Janice asked, "The process of what?"

Rowan considered his answer. "The process that tracks down a killer, and puts him in handcuffs, and takes him to jail. You know, crime and punishment."

"I see. Well then, tell Trooper Bateman I said *Hi*."

"Really?"

"No! *Not* really. Don't you dare."

Rowan shut off the phone and set it down. A few minutes later, Janice broached a different topic, "I think we should talk some more about your parents."

"Oh? Why?"

"Because you need to. Maybe I can help you with it. I know all about family dysfunction."

Rowan laughed ruefully. "Is that what it is?"

"Absolutely. Tell me: How much time did your parents actually spend with you?"

Rowan laughed. "As little as possible."

"You said they packed you off to boarding schools. Did you at least spend summer vacations together?"

"No. We didn't. There was an outdoor camp in north Georgia, near the foot of the Appalachian Trail; they sent me there every summer."

"For the whole summer?"

"Yes. Until it was time to go back to school."

"That's terrible."

"It was a family tradition. On the first day of school, my parents loaded the car with luggage, mine and theirs, and we drove off. They moved me into my new room at whatever school; then we had lunch somewhere where no one said anything; then they took off on a long trip—maybe to Brazil, or to Italy, or to New Zealand—and I didn't see or hear from them for months."

Janice asked, between clenched teeth, "When did this lovely family tradition start?"

"When they first sent me off to school."

"How old were you?"

"I don't know. Eight?"

"Eight!"

"And it continued all the way into college. They dropped me off at Appomattox College on day one, twenty years ago, and left. And that was the last time I ever saw them."

Janice didn't speak for a minute; then she asked him, "Okay. Why Appomattox College? That's pretty remote. And I had never heard of the place before."

"It was the only school that would take me. I had really bad grades."

"What if you didn't have bad grades? Where would you have gone?"

"I don't know. I always had bad grades."

Janice persisted. "Well, where did Doran go?"

"The University of Virginia."

"Ah. Ewell the Tool went there."

Rowan grimaced. "He did?"

"Yes. Briefly. My dad told me about it. He said Doran made some *huge* donation to UVA to get Ewell admitted. And he still managed to flunk out in his first year."

"Oh? I thought Ewell made it as far as law school."

"Sort of. After UVA, he got into Virginia Commonwealth. He hung on for four years there, and got a BA; but then he flunked out of the VC Law School."

Rowan sniggered, "I thought it was because he had mono."

"Yeah. Right. I think he still does." Janice turned her attention to driving for a minute. Then she resumed her questions. "What did you major in at Appomattox?"

Rowan shook his head. "Nothing really. I shouldn't be laughing at Ewell. I did worse. Much worse. I took courses—philosophy, religious studies, medieval studies—that sort of thing. But I rarely showed up for classes; I *never* showed up for exams so I failed them all."

"And they expelled you?"

"No. They should have, but they didn't." Rowan paused to collect his thoughts. Then he said, "Here's what happened: One night, so I have read, I had a psychotic episode. An acute one. My resident assistant—who, to my knowledge, was unaware of my existence— stated that I barricaded myself in my dorm room, perched myself on the window ledge, and jumped out."

"My God! Rowan!"

"But I don't remember doing that."

"Were you badly hurt?"

"I wasn't hurt at all! I fell three stories, about thirty feet, and started rolling down a hill. The RA and a campus security guard ran down the hill, and stopped me from rolling further, and held me there until an ambulance arrived. That's when my career as a mental patient began."

"Did they notify your parents?"

"They did. And they heard back, eventually. According to the written records, Doran Butler faxed in a form authorizing treatment. But I was already in treatment. I was in what they call *involuntary incarceration*."

"Involuntary? They can do that?"

"Oh yes. Different states have different names for it. In Virginia, it's called an ECO, an *Emergency Custody Order*. In Florida, it's called the *Baker Act*; in New York, it's *Kendra's Law*. Basically, they can lock you up if you pose a danger to yourself or others, especially if you've tried to kill yourself.

"Anyway, after two weeks of feeding me psychotropic drugs, my treatment was declared to be over. The ambulance drove me back to the dean's office, and that's when my career as a student came to an end. An ignominious one. The dean informed me that I had been expelled."

"And did this dean contact your parents?"

"I'm sure he tried to. But it didn't matter. I couldn't wait to get out of that place. The next morning, I left my dorm room, walked out the front door, and just kept on walking."

"What about your things?"

"What about them? They were irrelevant; just a closetful of preppy pants, shirts, and blazers. I left with whatever I had on. I walked into the woods, and I forded a shallow river, and I followed its course. I kept putting one foot in front of the other, walking in that river water all day. Near dusk, it got very cold, and my feet were freezing. I climbed up onto a dirt road by a peach orchard, and an old car pulled next to me and rolled down the window.

"It was Brother Abelard. He told me to get in, and I did, without question; without even thinking about it. He drove me to the Saint Francis Community for dinner. I was their guest for a week, and then I was a novitiate for six months, and then I became a full-fledged member."

"You became Brother Thomas."

"Yes. If he had not taken me in that night, I'd have just kept on walking, cold and wet, probably until I died."

Janice suggested, "So he saved your life?"

"Yes. Or he at least saved it that night. I'd say I saved my own life after that."

"How?"

"Through great effort. Through what I came to call my Three *R*s: *Repeating, Relaxing,* and *Reading*." He held up one finger and explained, "*Repeating* was the act of doing repetitive work, like making fruitcakes all day, every day, while praying in between."

"Three times a day."

"Yes. And always the same prayers, in the same order. Very easy for me."

"Because of the OCD."

"Yes." He added a finger and continued, "*Relaxing* was relaxing my mind. I did mindless tasks all day, with no pressure from teachers, or RAs, or deans. And my stress started to fade away."

"How long did that take?"

"It took a long time. I was really bad off. But I kept at it and, eventually, I cleared my head of a ton of junk. Many years' worth of junk."

"An entire childhood's worth."

"Yes."

"And what about reading?"

He raised up a third finger. "Reading? Well, that was a whole new thing for me. I was *not* a reader. Far from it. But one day, I drove with Brother Abelard to the county library. This was probably three years into my time at the Community. We were delivering fruitcakes for a fundraiser. He left me in the reading room, and I had a sort of epiphany. I sat there, surrounded by a thousand books, and I realized how few of them I had read; how little knowledge I had of life. So, then and there, I set myself on a new course, one of reading and learning."

Janice nodded. "Good for you."

"I only had a few hours a day to read, but I discovered that I had a gift for it. I could speed-read with full retention. I consumed at least one book a day for many years.

"Then, at some point, I had learned enough from books. I was ready to apply what I had learned to life. I was ready to leave the Community, but I had no idea how to do it, or where to go next. Newton's First Law of Motion says: *A body at rest tends to stay at rest, unless acted upon by an external force*. I was under the pull of a great inertia. I needed you, Miss Richman, to arrive in a blue car and set me back in motion."

Janice smiled. "Glad I could help." Then she whispered, "I miss my blue car."

Rowan told her, "You gave me my first ride in a convertible."

"I love that car."

"I read that my parents owned a convertible—in fact, they died in one—but I was never in it. And the Community never had one."

"What did they have again?"

"They had a car and a truck."

"Yeah. A Corolla and a Ranger?"

"That's right."

"And did you drive those?"

"No. I never did. Others did. They would take the Community's car and go off whenever they liked. As long as they filled in the sign-out sheet, and brought food back for Brother Abelard, he didn't care."

Janice shook her head. "Your parents never taught you to drive?"

"No. But I never wanted to. I still don't."

"Why?"

"It's too dangerous. And it pollutes the air."

Janice pointed out, "Not necessarily. You could get an electric car, a nice one. You could get a Tesla, *S*-class."

When he didn't respond, Janice switched the conversation back to her original topic. "Do you know what else is dangerous, Rowan? Grief. You can't keep it bottled up inside you. It's a killer. Not grieving for your parents, no matter how awful they were, can kill you. You have to close that circle and move on. If you don't, it can cause heart disease, diverticulitis, impotence."

Rowan conceded, "I know. I've read all that. I'm just not ready."

Janice said, "Okay. But can we at least talk about it some more?"

"Sure."

"Let's talk about the day you wandered off from Appomattox College. And the days that followed."

"All right."

"Didn't *someone* at the college wonder where you went? The RA? Or the dean? Or maybe your parents? Didn't anyone send out a search party when you just disappeared?"

Rowan pondered the question. He answered, "Well, the RA and the dean would not think I had disappeared. I was supposed to go home that day, so they would have assumed that I did."

"Okay. That leaves your parents."

"My parents were out of the country."

"But you said they were notified."

Rowan didn't respond for a time. Then he said quietly, "There is a report in the legal file. It's from a detective agency, the same one that MacDermott is using to spy on your father now. My parents *did* commission a search, but the search didn't turn up anything."

"The detectives didn't track you from the college to the Community?"

"No." He looked at her and added, "You're the only one who did that."

"So your parents just . . . concluded that you were dead? And moved on?"

"It sounds like it."

Janice sighed. "Oh, Rowan."

"Or maybe they thought I would just turn up some day, when I was good and ready." He smiled at her weakly, "And now I have."

Janice smiled back, but she didn't say much else for the next hundred miles. She fiddled with the radio while Rowan explored apps on his phone. In the early afternoon, the Ford Focus pulled over in front of the Richmond mansion. Rowan got out, stretched his arms, and then grabbed the shopping bag full of clothes from the back seat. He told Janice simply, "Thank you again. I'll see you tomorrow."

Janice replied, "Okay." Then she followed up with, "Don't you want to get dinner tonight?"

"No. I'd like to take some time to myself. If that's all right, I'm not used to all this . . . all this what?"

"Excitement?"

"Okay. Excitement. And there are some things I need to look into."

"Sure. All right. I'll see you in the morning then."

After pausing briefly in the lobby, Rowan entered his room and stripped down to his underwear and socks. He lay on top of the bed and dutifully performed his night-time ritual, hoping it would lead to a restful night's sleep. But it did not. He again slept fitfully, dreaming in fragments about his life at the Community, and at Appomattox College, and at his parents' dining room one Thanksgiving Day.

In the last dream fragment, he found himself looking up, from a child's seat at a children's table, into the blue eyes of a young woman with cascading red hair. The woman ladled cranberries onto his plate. Then she set the serving dish and ladle down and smiled at him. She opened her mouth to speak, and her lips moved, but the sound that came out was fleeting and incomprehensible, like a voice in a passing car. Rowan shook his head in frustration and woke up. He lay in the darkness, glancing around the room, re-orienting himself, marveling at the fact that tears were streaming down his face. He wiped his eyes with his hands; then he closed them and tried to return to the dream, but he could not.

Before dawn, Rowan slipped out the side door of the office building, dressed in his new clothes. He paused for a moment to observe a homeless man asleep behind the Dumpster. Then he turned and walked south for two miles, counting his steps, to the Oakwood Cemetery, the final resting place of his parents, as described in MacDermott's file.

Despite the early darkness and his unfamiliarity with the streets, he found the cemetery entrance easily. He was walking over a small hill, about fifty yards inside, when the sun broke the horizon. Once he crested the hill, he saw a newly dug gravesite. The site was sprawling, as large as any in the cemetery, and impressive to view, even in the faint light.

Rowan veered off a gravel path and stepped lightly on the dewy ground. He reached a pair of graves, still covered with mounds of dirt, and leaned over them. He bent to read the names on two tin markers: *Doran James Butler 1948-2018* and *Siobhan Kelly Butler 1969-2018*. From MacDermott's file, he knew that the tin markers were placeholders. His parents had bequeathed to themselves a granite monument, a monument still in its cutting and etching phases. When Rowan had seen the cost of the monument, three-quarters of a million dollars, it had astounded and then angered him. He had muttered to himself, in the silence of his bedroom, "So you *can* take it with you."

After a cursory look to the left and right, establishing that he was alone, he inclined his head and whispered, "But you never took *me* with you, did you? Why was that?" He ventured an answer. "Because I was a mistake? An embarrassment? A bastard?"

Rowan slowly lowered himself to his knees, feeling the mud seep through the material of his tan pants. He leaned forward until the elbows of his navy blazer were in the mud, too. He held that pose for a long moment. Then, to his own surprise, he started to weep again—

slowly at first, but soon in rivulets that ran to the middle of his face and then fell onto the ground.

When he was able to speak, he continued, "And to top it all off, I was defective. A defective little bastard. Unable to read like the other children; unable to get good grades from the teachers who wanted *nothing more* than to give me good grades; teachers who instead had to write reports about my weird behaviors."

Rowan sat back on his haunches and looked from Doran's grave to Siobhan's. He added, "And just when things couldn't get any worse . . . They did! I had a nervous breakdown, a psychotic episode. Nearly ruining one of your trips."

He held up three fingers to each of them in turn. "A bastard; a dunce; a nut-case. What an unholy trinity! So you kept your distance; you wrote me off; I understand."

Rowan straightened up and wiped his face with the top of his sleeve. He pushed himself up to a standing position and clapped mud and wet grass from his arms and hands. He retraced his steps to the gravel path, where he tried scraping his shoes clean on the rocks, but with little success.

He lifted his head toward the graves and opened his mouth to speak a peroration, but no words came out. No words even came to mind. So he turned away and trudged back up the cemetery path.

By nine AM, Rowan was standing outside the law offices waiting for Janice. He had peeled off the muddied clothes from the cemetery—shoes, socks, pants, and blazer—and stuffed them into a clear garbage bag. Then he dragged the bag out the side door and heaved it into the Dumpster, causing the homeless man to stir but not wake. To the obvious surprise of some passers-by, he was now wearing his brown monk's robe and sandals.

When Janice pulled up to the curb in front of him, she lowered the window and asked, "Rowan? What happened to your clothes?"

He answered simply, "They got dirty."

"What? All of them?"

"No. Not all of them." He looked down at his feet and explained, "It's just that . . . This outfit is more appropriate for today."

Janice started to protest, "Appropriate?" But then she caught herself and conceded, "Okay. If you say so." Then she added, "Do we have time for breakfast?"

Rowan nodded. He said, "At the same place?"

"Sure." Janice led the way across the street and into the luncheonette. She secured them a window table as on Monday. The smiling hostess handed them menus and, after brief consideration, they both ordered the same breakfast items.

Janice asked, "So what did you do last night? Did you enjoy your alone time?"

Rowan deflected the question. "I suppose. What did you do?"

"Me? I did what I always do. I called my girlfriends and bitched for two hours."

"Bitched?"

"Complained angrily."

"Oh? About what?"

"Mostly about our mothers."

Rowan replied absently, "Oh." But then he looked at her and said, "Actually, the truth is, I took your advice."

Janice widened her eyes. "You did? About what?"

"About grieving. About my parents. I went to the Oakwood Cemetery."

"When?"

"This morning, at first light."

"And?"

"And I grieved."

"And?"

"And I feel a little better now."

Janice nodded and replied, "Well, good."

"You know, in a way, I was complaining about my mother, too. And my father. But it was directly to them."

"Yes? Well, good for you."

Rowan paused to let a man from the kitchen set down their food. Then he resumed, "But . . . Why was that good? I was basically talking to two graves, to two piles of dirt."

She assured him, "Because it's not about *them*; it's about you. They did awful things to you, Rowan. They abused you. You were an abused child."

"An abused rich child?"

"Absolutely. I've dated guys with rich parents, and they had the expensive cars and the watches and all that, but they were damaged goods inside."

"Damaged by what?"

"By their mothers, more often than not. Sometimes by their fathers."

They stopped talking after that, except for some cursory remarks about the food. After they had finished eating, and were re-crossing Seventh Street, Janice turned to Rowan and asked, "So what is this meeting today about? Why did you want to gather everyone again?"

"It's not everyone."

"Don't get literal on me. Your family members? Your lawyers?"

Rowan added, with a touch of drama, "And my suspects."

Janice stepped up onto the curb and stopped. Her eyes widened as she asked him, "Your suspects? Really?"

He replied, "Yes."

"You have suspects?"

"Yes. I believe I know who killed Lance."

"You do?"

"Yes. And Steve Kowalski."

Janice hopped up and down in her high heels. "Oh! Can you tell me now?"

"No."

"Just me! I swear I won't say a word."

"No."

"Can you at least tell me: Was it the same person?"

Rowan started up the steps, so Janice followed. He told her, "Let's see how things play out. I believe that all will be revealed." They stopped in the outer office, where Rowan again took time to admire the ceiling mural. He asked, "Have you ever seen anything more beautiful?"

Janice conceded, "It is beautiful." She added, "The original, of course, is even more beautiful."

"I'm sure."

"And I have seen the original."

"You have? At Versailles?"

"Yes."

"The one in France?"

Janice laughed. "Yes. My dad took me there when I was eight."

"He took you to Paris?"

"He did. He took me lots of places." She swallowed hard. "Despite what my mother says, he was a good guy then; a good father. He wasn't always . . . like he is now."

Rowan asked, in a lowered voice, "And what about MacDermott? Was he always like he is now?"

Janice considered her answer. She replied in the same lowered voice, "I guess not. Not if he was once in love with Siobhan." Her voice dropped lower, into a conspiratorial whisper. "So! Was it Mister MacDermott? Did he try to kill you? Or did he order it done?"

Rowan asked her evenly, "What motive would MacDermott have?"

"I don't know. Sweet revenge?"

"Revenge for what? I've done nothing to him."

"No. But Siobhan did. She rejected him for someone else, for a cheating playboy, for someone he secretly despised. He couldn't get

163

back at Siobhan for that because Siobhan was dead. But he could get back at her only child."

Rowan conceded, "That's an interesting theory," but he said nothing else.

Janice prodded him, "People kill coldly, for revenge, and for money, but they also kill *hotly*, for passion."

Rowan asked, "Do you mean sexual passion?"

"Well, yes. That's the big one."

Rowan touched two fingers to his head, as if accessing a memory. He said, "We once had an incident in the Community; an incident of . . . of sexual passion, I guess you'd call it. A visitor, a guest resident, approached a young monk looking for sex."

"Really? Right there in the Community?"

"Yes. It happened there sometimes. We had all sorts of people coming in and out." He explained, "*Approached* may be too weak a word. This visitor crept over, in the dead of night, and lay down on top of the sleeping monk. The attacker was larger, and he had the element of surprise. He had his way with his young victim. It all happened in just a few seconds' time."

Janice said, "Sounds like P. E."

"What?"

"Premature Ejaculation. It's quite common. Please tell me that the young monk was not you, Rowan."

"It was *not* me. It was Brother John, a mild-mannered young fellow who slept in the bunk next to me."

"And you actually saw it happen?"

"Yes. I had just finished my night-time ritual, and I was lying still. I saw everything, and I heard everything."

"What did you do?"

"I waited until the attacker had crept back to his bunk, and had fallen asleep. Then I sat up to speak to Brother John, but no words ever left my mouth. They did not have to. He whispered to me right away, *Don't you worry, Brother Thomas. I already know what to do.*

"Brother John was renowned for his fine calligraphy. He was the one who would embellish the Perpetual Prayer cards."

Janice said, "Yes, I have seen his work."

Rowan continued, "He reached under his bed and pulled up a small bottle of black ink. He crept over to his sleeping attacker, and slowly poured the ink over the blackguard's face. The attacker sputtered for a moment, but he did not even wake up. It was not until the next morning, when the attacker saw the black ink on his pillow, and sheets, and felt it on his face, that he realized what had happened.

"He ran to the washroom and scrubbed mightily at the tell-tale stain with coarse soap, but it did not accomplish much. He appeared at Matins with the stain still on him; and at Mid-day Prayers, and at Vespers. No accusation was ever made, but it did not need to be. The man was stained for all to see. The next day, he walked out of the Community and never came back."

Janice started to reply, but she stopped when Charles MacDermott appeared, briefcase in hand, outside the glass doors. Rowan concluded with, "So today, we will be looking for a tell-tale stain."

MacDermott walked in and nodded curtly to Janice. He looked Rowan up and down and smiled broadly. He said, "I didn't know we were wearing costumes today."

"This is the robe of the Saint Francis Community."

MacDermott assured him, "I know, Rowan. I'm joking." He added, "So what is this meeting about?"

Rowan replied, "It's not a meeting. It's more of a question-and-answer session."

"Oh? Who is asking the questions?"

"I am."

MacDermott laughed mirthlessly. "You've come a long way in a week. In less than a week."

By way of reply, Rowan asked him, "Would you like to go first?"

"Pardon me?"

"Would you like to answer the first question? Now?"

MacDermott's laugh returned, but at half strength. He said, "Sure. Knock yourself out."

Rowan asked him, "What was your relationship with Siobhan Kelly?"

MacDermott pulled back. His tone changed from light to serious. He replied, "Are you referring to my late client, Missus Siobhan Butler?"

"No. I am referring to your secretary, Miss Siobhan Kelly. She was young; she was poor; she was ambitious."

MacDermott answered flatly, "What was our relationship? I was her boss; she was my employee."

"I see. Was she a good employee?"

"Yes, I'd say so."

"Was she a great employee?"

MacDermott shifted his briefcase from one hand to the other. "I don't know. The fact is, her duties were somewhat limited."

"Why is that?"

MacDermott responded with annoyance. "Because her education was limited. She was a high school girl who had taken a shorthand course."

"I see. So, what would she do for you, exactly?"

MacDowell pointed to the security camera. "She would do what your *movie machine* does now, Rowan, which is keep records. She would sit in meetings and take shorthand notes of whatever was discussed; then she would go off and type them up for me."

"Go off where?"

"Excuse me?"

Rowan answered with annoyance of his own. "These are simple questions. Where would she go to transcribe the shorthand notes?"

MacDermott pointed to the desk and swivel chair. "Right there. Same spot; same furniture." He then paused, pointed upward, and added, "She liked to sit and look up at that mural, I can tell you that much. She had seen it in a picture. From Versailles."

Rowan inquired dryly, "That's the place in France?"

"Yes. She mentioned it to Doran on one of his visits here. He was dropping in a lot back then, and I think it was to see her. Anyway, as the story goes: Siobhan told Doran on a Friday that she had seen a beautiful mural in a magazine. Then she pulled out a copy of *Paris Match* and showed it to him. He asked if he could borrow the magazine for the weekend, and she said *yes*, not thinking any more about it.

"But when she arrived at work on Monday, this mural was painted on the ceiling right above her head. Doran had paid some artist from Savannah some huge amount of money to come in here and replicate the mural. Siobhan was very impressed by that. Very moved, as I recall."

Rowan stared up and said, "I can see why. I love it. I love the blue sky."

MacDermott answered in a low voice, barely audible, "Yes. It was the blue of her eyes."

"Whose?"

"Siobhan's." He looked right at Rowan and then looked away. "I guess of your eyes, too."

The two men stared at each other in awkward silence. Then Rowan directed his finger at the swivel chair and inquired, "May I?"

"May you what?"

"Sit here?"

"Again, knock yourself out. Missus MacDermott is not here to stop you."

Rowan walked around the desk and sat tentatively on the chair, as if testing its weight limit. Then he swiveled slowly to the left, and right, and all around in a three hundred sixty-degree whirl.

MacDermott asked him, "Having fun?"

Rowan planted his feet and stopped. He said, "No. Not really. Do you think working here would be fun?"

MacDermott replied, "My wife seems to like it." He winked at Janice. "She thinks of herself as a partner now."

"My mother was *not* a partner, though. Was she? She was just the uneducated shorthand girl. Am I right?"

MacDermott sighed and muttered, "Okay."

"She was a scribe. Now, please do not ask me to repeat that. It is a simple word."

"A scribe?"

Rowan smacked his own head, "You did it anyway." Then he continued, "She *transcribed* documents for you, much like a medieval monk." MacDermott looked to Janice for help, but she avoided meeting his eyes.

Rowan went on. "Monks transcribed the Bible, by hand, for many centuries. It was how they made money, before the advent of prayer cards, and hand-hewn statues, and fruitcake."

MacDermott had heard enough. He answered dismissively, "Yeah. Fruitcake is right. I'm going in." He walked away, into the meeting room, where he took his familiar seat at the head of the table. A few seconds later, Rowan did the same, followed by Janice—both sitting to MacDermott's right, away from the door.

Rowan pointed to the laptop on the table and told Janice, "Thank you for arranging this."

Janice replied lightly, "Sure, *Mister iPhone*; now *Mister Laptop*."

Rowan said, "I explored some of its uses online. It's pretty simple."

She added, "*Mister High-tech*."

MacDermott pulled out an expanding file and set it on the table. He said, "Let's use this time to take care of some real estate business, Rowan. Have you decided to sell the three properties?"

"No."

"No, you haven't decided?"

"Oh, I've decided. I've decided to keep them."

MacDermott shook his head. He asked, "Why? To what possible purpose?"

"To live in. I will live in two of them."

"Two! Which two?"

"Charleston and Savannah."

MacDermott pointed to the walls around them. "Okay. And what about this one? Your Richmond property?"

"I have decided to turn this one into a home for veterans—veterans like my father, and like Steve Kowalski, and like the guy who stands outside rooting through the Dumpster. I contacted the Homeless Veterans Association yesterday afternoon, and they were very excited about the prospect. They have their own attorneys who will handle the transaction; who in fact are working on the transaction right now."

MacDermott sputtered, "What? You can't do that. This building isn't zoned for . . . a friggin' homeless shelter."

"I just read the zoning regulations online. Have you?"

MacDermott answered through gritted teeth, "Not lately."

"You should. You should also start packing up your things. It sounds like this transaction could happen quickly." He added, "To that end, U-Haul has already delivered a stack of boxes at the back door."

MacDermott fumed silently. Rowan and Janice fell quiet, too, until they heard the sounds of people arriving.

Kitty preceded Ewell and Mark Richman through the glass doors. She stomped into the meeting room with the others in tow. She looked at Rowan's robe and snapped, "Who are you supposed to be? Goddamn Darth Vader?"

Rowan met her gaze and explained flatly, "This is the robe worn by members of the Saint Francis Community."

"Oh? So you're going back there, where you belong?"

"No. I don't belong there anymore."

"You belong in a nut house!" Kitty looked at MacDermott, "What are we doing here? Are we getting our money today? Our so-called lawyer here won't tell us anything."

MacDermott started to respond, but Rowan cut him off. "We are not here to talk about lucre."

Kitty crinkled her face, causing deep lines to appear near her temples. "What? What the hell is luger?"

"*Lucre*. It's money, and we are not here to talk about it. We're here to talk about something more important." Kitty and Ewell exchanged a puzzled look; then each pulled out a chair and sat. Rowan went on, "We are here to talk about crime and punishment. About Cain and Abel."

Kitty asked the rest of the group. "He's a lunatic, right? A religious nut?"

Rowan continued calmly, "Since we last met in this office, two people have been murdered."

Mark Richman slid into the seat next to Janice. He was holding his head very level and still. Janice reached into her bag and pulled out a bottle of spring water and another of *Excedrin Extra Strength*. She opened the Excedrin and dumped two white caplets into her hand, offering the pills and water to her father. He seemed more annoyed than grateful, but he did take the pills and quickly washed them down with the water.

Rowan pointed to a broach on Kitty's lapel and commented, "I noticed that broach when you walked in today. I saw it on the divorce inventory."

"Yeah? So?"

"It's *sui generis*, is it not?"

Ewell sat up. He said, "Suing what? Who is suing who?"

Rowan answered, "*Sui generis*. It's Latin, Ewell."

Kitty snapped, "Don't start that crap again."

Rowan went on coolly. "The broach is one of a kind. It is *of its own genre. Or sui generis.*"

"Then say it in English, Nut-job. Do you think you're talking to goddamn Mexicans here?"

"The broach was given to your mother, Katherine Butler, by our mutual father, Doran Butler."

"Screw that! We don't have a mutual father."

But Ewell told her, "Actually, we do. According to the DNA test."

Kitty clamped her hand to her lapel, as if to fend off a robber. "This broach was our mother's! Now it's mine!"

Rowan explained, "According to the divorce papers, it was actually purchased for *my* mother, Siobhan Kelly, in Miami, for twenty-five thousand dollars."

"Your mother? Your mother was a little whore."

MacDermott broke in. "That's enough, Kitty!"

Rowan went on as if neither had spoken, "But the probate judge ruled that the broach was the mutual property of the divorcing couple. Therefore, Katherine Butler would get it."

Kitty answered triumphantly, "So it *is* mine!"

Rowan assured her, "Yes." Then he turned to her brother. "And I read in the same document that you, Ewell, received our mutual father's Diamond Rolex watch."

Ewell answered warily, "Yeah."

"Purchased in Geneva; valued at thirty-thousand dollars."

"Is that right?"

"Yes. Do you ever wear it?"

"No."

"Why?"

"Because it runs slow."

Rowan suggested, "Then you should get it fixed."

Ewell flopped out his hands and responded, "Yeah. But where?"

MacDermott interrupted again. "Rowan? Is this what you called us here for? To review inventory items?"

"No."

"Then can we please turn to the business at hand?"

Rowan shrugged. MacDermott pulled his chair in closer; he gestured around the table and said, "Then I am calling this meeting to order. Rowan, you requested a meeting of all parties, and all parties are present."

Rowan turned toward Janice's father, who was sitting very still and erect, but with his eyes closed. He asked, "Mister Richman, are you present?"

Mark Richman opened his eyes slowly and answered, "Obviously."

Janice produced a tissue, reached over, and dabbed at the pools of water on his lower eyelids.

Rowan told him, "Good. Because I want to begin with you."

Mark Richman raised his left hand, indicating that his daughter should stop what she was doing. Janice pulled back the tissue, and he said, "Begin with me . . . to what?"

"To identify the killer."

MacDermott held out both hands. "Come on. Seriously? *That's* what this meeting is about?"

Rowan replied, "Yes."

"Shouldn't we be leaving that to the police?"

"The police have their process; I have mine."

MacDermott scoffed, "*You're* going to identify the killer?" He shot a look at Janice, "I've heard you can't even identify common objects."

Janice held up her index finger and wagged it at her boss. "I said that earlier in the week, Mister MacDermott. I don't say it now. It turns out he's an incredibly fast learner."

Rowan told MacDermott, "Yes. I have learned some things. Fast. I've read everything that's available; I've talked to everyone involved; I've observed what's to be observed." He paused, then added, "And I've drawn some conclusions."

MacDermott nodded warily. He answered, "Fine. Let's hear them."

Rowan looked around the table. He said, "Let 's begin with the *prima facie,* literally, the *first face* of these sad events." Rowan looked at Ewell, who looked back vacantly. "There have been two attempts on my life since we last met. And two innocent men have died. Lance Myers was first. His misfortune was to be sitting in Janice's car, the car I had been sitting in earlier that day."

MacDermott asked, "Is he the gay one?"

"Yes. He had dyed his hair red, and it looked like mine. That proved to be a fatal decision. Steve Kowalski was second. He was the victim of unfortunate circumstances as well: He was wearing my clothes, and he was sitting in my garden."

MacDermott inquired again, "He's the homeless one? On the bench?"

"Yes. The conclusion is obvious: *I* was the killer's target both times. So then I had to ask: *Who might try to kill me? Twice?*"

Rowan turned his attention to the sweating Mark Richman. "Someone who had much to lose, professionally, when I turned out to be alive? Mister Richman, your clients Kitty and Ewell were denied the fortune that you implied would be theirs."

Mark Richman protested, "I never said that."

"No. But you implied it, which was good enough for them to start counting up their earnings." He looked at them and added, "Counting their chickens."

Kitty raised one middle finger in his direction, and Rowan resumed. "You are a man with a drinking problem, sir. A man who is perhaps delusional; who perhaps thinks no one can see him drowning in a vat of liquor."

Janice spoke, as if at an intervention. "Everyone *can* see that, Dad. Everyone knows you have a problem."

Rowan continued, "You are a man who admits to having blackouts. And, most damning of all, you are a man who can be placed at my house, at the scene of the second murder, on the very day of the crime."

Mark Richman hung his head. He didn't say a word. His hands flipped forward, extending from his blue suit as if waiting to be put into handcuffs.

But Rowan concluded, "And yet, you could not have done it."

Mark Richman looked up at him, bleary-eyed.

"Let's discuss the murders in reverse order. At the request of Trooper Bateman, the Charleston police brought you in for questioning about the one in my garden. They dusted your hands for gunpowder but found none; not a trace.

"And as to the first murder in Richmond? Mister MacDermott's detectives were following you on the night of that one, as they have been for two weeks. They recorded your movements in fifteen-minute increments. You *were* in a bar on the night that Lance Myers was murdered, but it was up in Northside, nowhere near the *Virginia Squire*."

Mark Richman pulled in his hands and folded them one over the other.

Rowan looked across the table. "That brings me to your clients, your very angry clients, Kitty and Ewell."

Kitty snarled, "We don't have to listen to this."

"My siblings here—"

"Half-siblings, you bastard!"

Rowan corrected himself, "My half-siblings. Yes. I'm afraid you two must share the spotlight as Suspect Number Two. Let's call you each a half-suspect. Kitty and Ewell had the most to gain, of course, if I were to . . . stop living. But I can quickly eliminate them due to one simple fact: Attempting a murder is difficult. Attempting it again the next day is doubly so. Neither of you is capable of attempting anything difficult—of persevering when something proves to be hard—such as having a heel fixed on a Jimmy Choo shoe, or getting a Diamond Rolex watch repaired."

Kitty snarled, "Screw you, you monk-bastard-piece of shit!" while Ewell stared down at his own wrist.

Rowan leaned back and looked to his left. "So who does that leave?" MacDermott's lip rose in a snarl. Rowan said, "Let's put it this way: *He is the type of person who would hire a detective to follow his own partner around in order to gather dirt on him.*"

MacDermott answered, "You bet your ass I would. If he was ruining my business!"

"He is also the type of person who would brag to me that he knew people—*less-than-reputable people*—who got things done. Might he have hired such people to follow me in Janice's car? Might his hired killers have mistaken me for a man with red hair on one night, and for a man in a Brooks Brothers suit the next day? Perhaps."

MacDermott warned him, "You're making serious allegations here."

"I am."

"You're slandering people."

"I am only slandering people if what I say is false or malicious. Isn't that the legal standard, Ewell?"

Ewell, pleased to be brought into the conversation, answered enthusiastically. "Yes!"

MacDermott reasserted himself. "What evidence do you have? What can you prove?"

Rowan sighed. He answered, "I have evidence, but it proves that you, too, are innocent." He added, "Of this crime, at least."

Rowan reached over and opened the lid of the laptop. He maneuvered the mouse, and clicked on an icon. Then he turned the screen and pulled it back toward his chest so all could see.

The first image to come into view was the face of Brother Abelard, and he appeared to be dozing. Rowan bent over the laptop and raised his voice. "Brother Abelard! Brother Abelard!"

The abbot opened his eyes, blinked, and stared out from the screen. He said, "Ah, Brother Thomas!" Then he added, "We have been praying for your parents, Brother; for Siobhan and Doran Butler, three times a day."

"Yes. I appreciate that." Rowan explained, "I requested to see you at this time of day, Brother—the time between Matins and Mid-day Prayers—so that it would not interrupt the routine too much. I hope it is convenient for you."

"Certainly. Yes."

"How have you been, Brother Abelard?"

"I have been missing *you*, Brother Thomas, and your many talents. When might we expect you back?"

Rowan smiled. "I would say *never*, but there is an aphorism that warns us to never say that."

"I shall hold out hope, then." The abbot appeared to look deeper into the screen. "Tell me: Who else is there with you?"

Rowan tilted the laptop and panned the group. "Well, there are my long-lost, and just-re-met, half-siblings. That's a lot of hyphens, isn't it?"

"Ah."

Kitty rolled her eyes; Ewell stared blankly.

Rowan panned further. "Then there are the attorneys-at-law. Two more hyphens."

"I see."

Rowan tilted the laptop to his left. "Then there is Janice."

"Ah! Miss Richman. Yes, I remember you."

Janice gave him a subdued wave. "Hello, Abbot."

"I remember the day you came out here and pried our Brother Thomas away."

"Is that what I did?"

"Yes. You were very persistent. Others were not."

Rowan set the laptop back down and asked, "Others? There were others, Brother?"

"Oh yes. A long time ago. Some prying people came here, from some agency, to inquire about you. It was by your secular name, of course."

Rowan looked to Janice and then back. "Detectives came to you, to inquire about me, twenty years ago, and you told them I was not there?”

“I told them that no one named Rowan Butler was here.”

“And they went away?”

“Yes. Like I said, they were not persistent.”

Rowan put his head down and thought about the abbot’s words. He looked up and said softly, to no one in particular, “There is a Bible quote for that: *Everything has its own time.*”

Bother Abelard answered, “Yes, indeed! It was not your time to leave.”

“Apparently.”

“I know that verse! Ecclesiastes, Chapter Three, Verse One. Is it not?”

Rowan affirmed, “It is.”

Brother Abelard nodded enthusiastically and repeated, “Everything has its own time.” Then he asked, “Tell me: What is it time for today?”

Rowan exchanged a quick look with Janice. Then he began, “It is time for justice, Brother. I hope. I have contacted you because two people, two new acquaintances of mine, have just died.”

“Oh? And are these people who would benefit from our perpetual prayers?”

“Perhaps, Brother. I think we all could benefit from that. But we must discuss that at a later time. For now, I want to tell you, and the others siting here with me, who caused those two deaths.”

Brother Abelard’s face drooped with sorrow. “So they did not die by natural causes?”

“No. The sad fact is, Brother, that both were murdered in cold blood.”

“Ah! That is shocking.”

Rowan went on, “As you know, Brother Abelard, I am an early riser. I am always up and out before first light.”

“Indeed you are.”

"The other day, I awoke early and walked out into the street, among the street people. I was a rich man walking among the poor; a man with three homes walking among the homeless. They were wary of me at first, but eventually, they started talking to me."

Janice interrupted. "Rowan? Did you give them money?"

He admitted, "I distributed some twenty-dollar bills, yes."

"*That's* why they talked to you."

Rowan conceded, "Perhaps. I don't know. I do know that *two* of them remembered vehicles parked near the Charleston mansion on the day of the murder, vehicles with out-of-state plates. One talked about an older car; another about a small truck. They didn't remember much about them—like where the plates were from—but they both remembered this: The vehicles were stained red; they had red clay caked along the bottom, a red clay that was not from around there. It was a clay that you and I know well, Brother Abelard."

Brother Abelard spoke up. "The peaches grow best in red clay."

"They do."

"They make the finest fruitcake."

"Perhaps. I don't really know. I do know this: Murder is evil, and evil leaves a stain. Sometimes it is a black ink stain; sometimes it is a red clay stain; sometimes it is a gunpowder stain."

Janice picked up her ears when she heard an off-camera voice. A man now spoke to Rowan: "Like you said, Mister Butler, both of them had black powder stains on their hands. The residue was clearly visible under a violet light."

Janice gasped, "Is that Trooper Bateman?"

Rowan affirmed, "It is."

"Whose hands is he talking about?"

Trooper Bateman entered the frame slowly, squeezing Brother Abelard to the right and then completely out of view. Everyone in the meeting room leaned forward to see who Trooper Bateman had with him. It was someone in handcuffs, and Janice blurted out his name, "Brother Carl!"

Brother Carl stared at the laptop, twisting his head, trying to identify who was on the other side. He leaned in so that the top half of his face filled the screen, showing his two rolling eyeballs. Then he pulled back, revealing that the neck of his brown robe was torn, and his black toupee was askew, as if it he had been in a scuffle. He snarled, "Brother Thomas, is that you?"

Rowan replied, "It is. And some others."

Brother Carl sneered, "It's Friday, Brother Thomas! You know what that means for us, right?"

Rowan answered evenly, "It means it's a baking day."

"Yeah. We're baking fruitcakes today. We'll be shipping them out tomorrow, to people who don't really want them. But we don't care. Do we?"

When Rowan did not reply, Brother Carl snapped, "No! We don't! So everybody had better deal with it! We're shipping them out anyway, because that's what we do."

Rowan started to speak, "Brother Carl—"

But the angry monk shouted over him, "But *you* don't care about fruitcake, do you? You OCD nut-job! You don't care about anything but yourself!"

Rowan replied evenly, "Oh, I care about some things. I care about two people who are no longer alive because someone thought they were *me*. Because someone thought *I* should be dead." Rowan raised his voice, "Brother Abelard? Do you have the sign-out sheets?"

The big abbot came back into view, positioning himself behind Brother Carl and Trooper Bateman. He held up a pair of clipboards and nodded.

Rowan asked him, "Can you tell me who signed out the Toyota Corolla on Tuesday night, the night of Lance Myers' murder?"

The abbot answered, "Brother Carl signed out the car that night, and he signed it out the next day, too."

Rowan said, "Yes. I thought of Brother Carl when I saw the bullet pattern on the wall at the *Virginia Squire*. I've seen such scatterings of shot against the Community's barn, and against the residence hall, and even against the back of the church; wherever Brother Carl had stopped to shoot at an evening meal. The pattern was not as evident on the garden wall in Charleston, but if you looked hard, between the lichen stains, you could see it.

"Trooper Bateman informs me that, in both cases, the victim had been wounded by the buckshot, but not killed. The victim had been able to move, and perhaps had attempted escape, only to be stopped with a coup de grace."

Brother Carl leaned forward again and spoke with complete sincerity. "I just wanted to see for myself that it was true, Brother Thomas. That I had been screwed to a divine level. That some red-haired whacko, who has shoveled shit with me for the last twenty years; who has to count every step when he walks; who has to go all ninja-yogi with every muscle before he can go to sleep, has inherited millions of dollars, while I remain penniless. I just had to see that cosmic joke for myself, in all of its beauty."

Rowan expressed his bewilderment. "And *that* led you to attempt murder? To attempt two murders?"

The little man blinked. He replied, "What do you mean? *Attempt?*"

Rowan told him, "As with most things, Brother, you did not succeed. But the attempts will have serious consequences nonetheless." Rowan turned his attention to the arresting officer. "Trooper Bateman? Can we proceed?"

Trooper Bateman looked off-camera and nodded, and a uniformed arm pulled Brother Carl out of the frame. The trooper then guided a second brown-robed figure into view. It was Janice again who provided the name, "Sister Agnes?"

Rowan prompted the abbot, "Brother Abelard? Do you know what I'm going to ask now?"

Brother Abelard raised the clipboards again. "Yes. Sister Agnes signed out the Ford Ranger on Tuesday and Wednesday. That made me suspicious, since both she and Brother Carl signed out the vehicles two days in a row, and they were both gone for a long time, and neither came back with any supplies. When they tried to sign out the vehicles for a third time, I told them both *No*."

Rowan turned to the others in the meeting room. "You see, Brother Carl believes he committed those two murders. He certainly tried, which is a serious crime, but the fact is that he tried and failed. Two times. Sister Agnes, tailing him in the pickup, finished the job for him. Two times. Each crime scene featured a blast from a shotgun that had scattered buckshot but had killed no one. Each murder victim actually died from a seven-millimeter cartridge through the head. Fired from a Remington Seven Hundred rifle. A coup de grace."

Trooper Bateman clicked a second pair of handcuffs onto Sister Agnes, commenting, "You were right, Mister Butler: *Hell hath no fury like a woman scorned*. She had gunpowder residue on both hands."

The little nun stared down at the handcuffs. She kept her gaze downward as she muttered, in a voice devoid of any emotion, "Brother Thomas, you took a vow. You broke it."

Rowan answered, "You broke a commandment, Sister. The fifth one: *Thou shalt not kill*."

Sister Agnes did not react at first, other than to repeat quietly, as if reciting a prayer, "You took a vow. You broke it." But then, very slowly, she raised her head and craned her neck to look into the laptop. Her eyes scanned the meeting room until she found Janice. Then they stopped. She snarled, "You wouldn't break a vow for me, Brother. No! Heaven forbid. But you'd break one for her in a minute."

Then she fell silent, retracting her head and neck like a turtle's. When it became apparent that she would not be speaking again, Trooper Bateman turned the little nun to her right and guided her out of the frame. This left only Brother Abelard. The abbot shook his large head. "I am terribly sorry, Brother, that we—we here at the Community—were involved in the loss of two lives."

Rowan said, "I don't fault you, Brother. You saved a *third* life, most likely mine, when you didn't let them take the vehicles on that third day. I felt a sense of dread that day, all day long."

Janice said, "So did I."

Rowan added, "So thank you for that."

The abbot replied, "You needn't thank me, Brother. It was God's providence at work."

Rowan nodded, but he did not speak, and the big man left the frame.

The observers in the meeting room, however, remained riveted on the laptop for another two minutes as they listened to the sound of other police officers taking over, clicking and unclicking handcuffs, reading Miranda rights, taking statements.

Finally, when he was satisfied that the proceedings were over, Rowan looked from Janice to his half-siblings to his lawyers, and said, "Well, that is that." He then added, "Except for one bit of housekeeping." He informed them all: "When you leave here today, it will be for the last time. These offices, the Law Offices of MacDermott and Richman, are now officially closed."

Ewell looked at the lawyers and then at Rowan. He blinked and asked, "What? What's happening to the law offices?"

"I am turning this building into a home for veterans. For homeless veterans."

Ewell attempted to restate. "You're selling the building to veterans?"

"No. No, I'm *giving* it to them."

"Why?"

"Because they need it."

Kitty said, "Because he's a nut-case, Ewell! A nut-case who thinks he's Darth Vader." She rounded on Rowan. "And he'll always be a nut-case! Giving shit away? Walking around in a dress? Talking in Pig Latin? He'll wind up in a fucking loony bin yet, and we'll get our money. If there's anything left of it."

Kitty then yelled at her brother, "Get up, Ewell! Let's get out of here." She led Ewell to the door. She turned back to Rowan and warned him, "This isn't over, you little shit-bastard, crazy bastard . . . bastard."

Mark Richman watched them leave. He made no move to join them. After they hade cleared out, he told Janice, "Those pills helped. Thank you."

Janice patted his hand. "Good."

He looked at MacDermott and said, "It sounds like we should pack up our things."

MacDermott pressed his fingers against his closed eyelids and muttered, "This cannot be happening." But he did get out of his chair, and he did gesture to Mark to precede him out of the room. They walked through the front office, turned right, and disappeared down the back hallway.

Rowan started to close the lid of the laptop, but he stopped upon hearing Trooper Bateman say, "Miss Richman? Are you still there?"

Janice exchanged a puzzled look with Rowan and answered, "Yes. I'm here."

The trooper entered the frame and said, "Good. I have some information about your vehicle."

"Oh? Yes?"

"Yes. Our body repair guy back at the barracks tells me there's nothing wrong with the car internally; it's all external. Chewed-up tires; bullet holes on the side and back. He'll need to replace those panels and then re-paint the car, but it's all fixable. It's *not* totaled."

Janice smiled and replied, "Great. So when can I get it back?"

"Well, unfortunately, your car is evidence in a homicide investigation. That can take time."

"Oh."

"But Brother Carl and Sister Agnes are both admitting their guilt. He will be charged with attempted homicide, two counts; she will be charged with homicide, two counts. Guilty pleas do speed up the process. So, a month maybe?"

"Okay. I'm okay driving the Ford Focus for a month. It's just that it's . . . not my car."

"Yeah. I hear you. I feel the same way about my ride."

They stopped talking after that, and an awkward silence ensued. Trooper Bateman finally said, "Okay, Miss Richman. I'll be signing off then."

Janice replied, "Okay. Take care," and started to close the laptop lid, until she realized that the sound was still on. She turned to Rowan, put her finger to her lips, and leaned in closer. They heard Brother Abelard say, "Here you are, Trooper. Now remember to bury him upside down, facing the house."

Janice could not control herself. She blurted out, "What? What are you talking about?"

Trooper Bateman's face popped back into view; nonplussed; upset that the screen and microphone were still active. Janice asked him, "What did you do?" to which he replied weakly, "Nothing."

"Don't tell me you bought a Saint Joseph statue!"

As they faced off, Rowan drifted out of the room to afford them some privacy. He stopped at the black chair, his mother's chair, and sat. He slowly rotated left; then right, and then in a full circle. He leaned back as far as he dared in the swivel seat, and looked up at the painted ceiling.

He heard Janice say, "How could you?" and the trooper answer, "What? My mom's trying to sell her place."

"That's not going to help!"

"But it can't hurt."

"You should be ashamed."

The trooper conceded, "All right. Tell you what: I'll be half-ashamed. How's that?"

Janice giggled.

Rowan got up from the chair. He walked down the hallway, intending to go to his bedroom, but he changed his mind upon hearing the sounds of MacDermott and Richman packing up their belongings. He exited the building through the back door, turned the corner, and peered into the alcove looking for sleepers.

Seeing none, he turned back and walked to a spot directly under the fire escape ladder. He stood there, somewhat bewildered. He considered the fact that, for the first time in his life, he had nowhere to go and nothing to do. After a moment, he stretched to his full height and reached up, grasping the bottom-most rung of the ladder. He pulled it down and climbed, hand over hand, to the landing on the second floor; then he climbed to the landing on the third floor, and finally up to the gravel rooftop. He crunched over the stones, counting each step, until he reached a low wall. He saw that he was facing south, toward the Oakwood Cemetery and a pair of freshly dug graves. After long consideration, he mumbled two prayers for his parents— an *Our Father* and a *Hail Mary.*

Then he turned away and crossed, steadily and noisily, to another side of the roof, to another wall. He stared west, up a city street controlled by red lights and green lights, trying to visualize the St. Francis Community going about its business just a half-day's drive away. It seemed so distant now; a distant memory of Matins, and Mid-days, and Vespers, the red lights and green lights that had controlled his life for all those years. Those calls to prayer had been his boundaries, but they were now gone. Gone for good. Leaving him here, on his own, staring down at a boundless new world.

9 781966 196488